The Christmas Project

The Royal Kensington Hospital's jet-set Christmas!

It's no secret that Christmas is the most wonderful time of the year! But for four of the Royal Kensington Hospital's top medical staff, this festive season will be one for the books... Why? They've just been invited to take part in the London hospital's prestigious Kensington Project!

With their passports in hand, the Royal Kensington Hospital's best and brightest are ready to share their specialist expertise—and the holiday season—with hospitals around the world. From Jamaica to New York, Toronto to Sweden, they're prepared to face busy wards and heart-pounding emergencies. But a pulse-racing encounter or two under the mistletoe? No one included that in the Kensington Project's handbook! The expert team may be giving the gift of the Kensington Project this year...but will they receive the greatest gift of all— happily-ever-after?

Christmas Miracle in Jamaica
by Ann McIntosh

December Reunion in Central Park
by Deanne Anders

Winter Nights with the Single Dad
by Allie Kincheloe

Festive Fling in Stockholm
by Scarlet Wilson

Available now!

Dear Reader,

Anyone who knows me knows that I love writing a Christmas story, so when Carly, my editor, asked if I wanted to take part in the Royal Kensington Hospital Christmas series it was an instant yes! Not only did I get to work with three other fabulous medical authors, I also got the wonderful city of Stockholm as my Christmas setting.

I had great fun learning all about Stockholm and sending my hero and heroine, Jonas and Cora, all around the city to help them find their happily-ever-after.

I hope you'll enjoy reading the story as much as I enjoyed writing it.

Love,

Scarlet Wilson

A FESTIVE FLING
IN STOCKHOLM

———

SCARLET WILSON

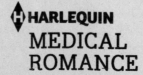
HARLEQUIN
MEDICAL
ROMANCE

Special thanks and acknowledgment are given to Scarlet Wilson for her contribution to The Christmas Project miniseries.

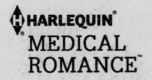

HARLEQUIN®
MEDICAL
ROMANCE™

Recycling programs
for this product may
not exist in your area.

ISBN-13: 978-1-335-40894-5

A Festive Fling in Stockholm

Harlequin Enterprises ULC
22 Adelaide St. West, 40th Floor
Toronto, Ontario M5H 4E3, Canada
www.Harlequin.com

Printed in U.S.A.

Scarlet Wilson wrote her first story at age eight and has never stopped. She's worked in the health service for twenty years, having trained as a nurse and a health visitor. Scarlet now works in public health and lives on the West Coast of Scotland with her fiancé and their two sons. Writing medical romances and contemporary romances is a dream come true for her.

Books by Scarlet Wilson

Harlequin Medical Romance

Double Miracle at St. Nicolino's Hospital
Reawakened by the Italian Surgeon

Changing Shifts
Family for the Children's Doc

London Hospital Midwives
Cinderella and the Surgeon

The Good Luck Hospital
Healing the Single Dad's Heart
Just Friends to Just Married?

Tempted by the Hot Highland Doc
His Blind Date Bride

Visit the Author Profile page
at Harlequin.com for more titles.

This Christmas story is dedicated to my two weddings of 2021, Dillon and Megan Glencross, and Stuart and Carly Walker. Two beautiful brides and two gorgeous grooms—wishing you all the love in the world

Praise for
Scarlet Wilson

"[C]harming and oh so passionate, *Cinderella and the Surgeon* was everything I love about Harlequin Medicals. Author Scarlet Wilson created a flowing story rich with flawed but likable characters and… will be sure to delight readers and have them sighing happily with that sweet ending."

—*Harlequin Junkie*

Scarlet Wilson won the 2017 RoNA Rose Award for her book
Christmas in the Boss's Castle

CHAPTER ONE

CORA CAMPBELL WALKED briskly down the long corridor of the Royal Kensington Hospital, wondering if biting her nails might be an option. Her pager had already sounded twice.

As a neonatologist she'd spent the last twelve years of her life listening to the sound of a pager—at some stages it had almost dictated her life. Usually she welcomed it. It meant she was needed. She would be busy. She would be serving the tiny patients to whom she'd dedicated her life. But this time was different. This time it was Chris Taylor, the chief executive of her hospital, paging her, and her stomach was doing uncomfortable flip-flops.

She had to be in trouble.

The long walk wasn't helping. It was giving her lots of time to contemplate all the trouble she could be in. She'd signed for new state-of-the-art incubators last week. She'd authorised two extra staff to work over Christmas, because the same old faces went 'off sick' every year at that time. She promised one remote teaching session a week with a prestigious US hospital. She'd just had her fifth professional paper published on a new pioneering technique she'd introduced last year for neonates between thirty-one and thirty-three weeks. The before and after was quite astonishing, and right now she was wondering if the before had unintentionally shown the hospital in a bad light.

She glanced down as she neared the office. Maybe she should have gone back to her locker and put some heels on for a more professional look? Cora always tried to be dressed in a presentable manner at work, comfortable black trousers, a short-sleeved unfussy red top and her trademark shoes. A fellow doctor had introduced her to them at the conference in the US: flat, and completely machine washable, they were as comfortable as slippers and came in a rainbow of colours—all of which Cora had promptly purchased. They were also a dream when running the miles of corridors to an emergency page.

'Hey, Cora.'

Lucy, the chief executive's PA, was sitting behind her desk beaming like the Cheshire Cat. This didn't look like the sign of trouble.

'How's Louie?' Cora asked automatically. 'Can I see a photo of my favourite boy?'

Lucy grabbed her phone from her bag and immediately turned it to face Cora. Her son Louie had been born at twenty-six weeks, two years previously. Cora had looked after him, and always liked to check on his progress.

A sticky face and wide smile beamed up at her. Louie had a shock of blond hair, and a twinkle in his eye. He was also holding a crayon and had clearly just drawn on a white wall.

'Oh, no! The cheeky wee devil. When was that?'

'Sunday,' Lucy said with a smile as she stuffed the phone back in her bag. 'The decorator had just finished the hallway, and Louie decided he wanted to decorate too.' She shook her head. 'I swear, I just turned my back for second. He'd been sitting right next to me eating a yoghurt.'

Cora laughed and nodded. 'What can I say? He's just trying to keep you on your toes.' She winked at her. 'We teach them lots of tricks in NICU.'

She knew Lucy had worried endlessly about her early arrival. But although Louie was still a little small, he was meeting all his milestones with bells on. Cora shifted on her feet and glanced at the closed door. 'So, spill, am I in trouble?'

Lucy widened her eyes, in the way that only a person who knew everyone's secrets could. 'Dr Campbell, what on earth could you be in trouble for?' There was an edge of humour to her mocking tone.

Cora shrugged. 'I thought of nearly half a dozen reasons on the way down the corridor. You really should persuade him to move office. It would be much better for my fear factor if he were situated right next to the stairs.'

Lucy laughed and shook her head as the intercom on her desk sounded. 'That's for you.' She gave her a wink. 'And I don't think you've got anything to worry about.'

Cora sucked in a deep breath and walked over to the door, giving it two knocks before she pushed it open and stepped inside.

Chris Taylor rose to his feet and extended his hand towards her. Cora was immediately struck by the enormous window and the view of London outside. Even though she'd worked at the Royal Kensington for years she'd only ever been in this office on a few occasions. She smiled nervously and shook his hand. 'I would never get any work done in here. I'd be too busy people watching.'

His normally serious face broke into a smile

as he shook his head. 'I don't believe that for a second. You never stop working, Dr Campbell.' He lifted something from his desk. 'As your newly published peer-reviewed paper demonstrates.'

Darn. He'd read it. That must be why she was here. 'Oh, about that. I don't think you should concentrate too much on the before. The Royal Kensington still demonstrated an excellent level of care.'

One eyebrow arched. 'As I would expect,' he said smoothly.

Cora fought the urge to clear her throat and shift in her seat, conscious it would make her look guilty of something. Chris Taylor placed the medical journal back on his desk and clasped his hands in front of him. This was it. This was the position he frequently assumed in press conferences when he was about to deliver news.

'Dr Campbell, I invited you here today in part—' he nodded his head at the journal '—because of your latest publication, and in part, because of an offer I'd like to make to you.'

An offer? Cora immediately straightened in her chair, every cell of her body on alert. An offer was good—right?

'You've been with us a while, so I take it you've heard of the Kensington Project?'

Cora almost choked. 'Yes, of course.' Everyone who worked at the Royal Kensington knew about the Kensington Project.

It was obviously the correct answer because Chris gave a gracious smile. 'You know that we think of ourselves as being home to the best and brightest in the world. Every year we send four of our pioneering team members out to train staff in other hospitals across the world. This year, we'd like you to be one of those members.'

Something was wrong. Her skin was tingling as if a million centipedes were marching over it. Her mouth had just decided she was stuck in the Sahara Desert, and the thirty-three years of knowledge and experience her brain stored had just vanished in a puff of a magician's wand.

Chris was obviously waiting for some kind of response.

She'd wanted this. She'd wanted this for the last few years, and last year had been sadly disappointed when she'd heard that four others had been selected. She'd gone to a nearby bar with her good friend Chloe and they'd both had a glass of wine to commiserate.

This year though, between her teaching,

her research paper, and the maternity leave of a colleague, she hadn't even had a chance to watch the calendar and wonder when the announcements might be made.

Chris was still patiently looking at her, as red London buses and black cabs whizzed by outside.

'Fabulous.' It came out almost as a squeak.

Satisfied, he continued. 'We've had a request from…' he consulted a list on his desk '… Stockholm City Hospital in Sweden. They'd like you to train a wide range of their neonatal staff on the pioneering techniques you developed while working at the Royal Kensington.'

She heard the hidden unspoken message. They might be her techniques, but credit would always have to be given to the hospital that had supported her. Cora didn't mind. The Royal Kensington had frequently put their money and trust in her over the last few years, when she'd outlined plans for improvement, both small and large. Her success rate was good. And even when a few things hadn't quite achieved their goal, there had always been learning for all those involved.

Excitement fizzed down inside her. This was an honour. A privilege to visit another country and teach them first-hand all the techniques she'd learned. Stockholm. Sweden. She'd never been to either before and that added even more to the excitement.

Chris kept talking. 'If you choose to accept, then you'll leave in three days' time—the first of November.'

'Three days?' If he heard the note of alarm in her voice, Chris Taylor showed no sign of acknowledgement.

'The arrangements are in place. You'll be flying into Arlanda Airport and we've arranged for you to be picked up and taken to your accommodation. You'll be there for just over seven weeks, flying home on Christmas Eve. I trust these arrangements will be suitable?'

Cora nodded. Her brain was kicking back into gear and she had a million questions.

'Who will I be working with? Do I get to take any of my equipment?' She frowned. 'How do I transport hospital equipment? Where will I be staying? Who are the others involved in the Kensington Project this year?' She paused to catch her breath. 'You said they requested me? Is that usual? Is that how this normally works?'

She caught the gleam in Chris Taylor's eyes and realised exactly how she must sound.

She gave a short laugh and a shrug. 'What's the weather like in Stockholm?'

There was silence for a few moments and Chris tilted his head to one side. 'Is that a yes, Dr Campbell?'

She jumped to her feet as he stood and held out his hand again. 'Yes!' she said, shaking his hand with an overenthusiastic grip. 'That's definitely a yes.'

He smiled. 'In that case, Lucy has a number of details for you that she prepared earlier. I think it's safe to say you're in very good hands.'

Cora didn't doubt it for a second. Lucy was meticulous with her work.

She let his hand go and moved back to the door. 'Thank you. Thank you. I'll check the rota. I'll need to make sure there's enough cover at short notice. I'll speak to Ron in Medical Physics about the transport and review all my patients.'

As her hand closed on the door handle she realised she was babbling again.

'Dr Campbell?'

Chris's amused voice came from behind her. She looked over her shoulder. 'Yes?'

He glanced at her red flats. 'Buy some winter boots.'

'I have wonderful news!' The door to Jonas Nilsson's office burst open with a bang and

Elias Johansson came into the room, his eyes sparkling and his smile wide.

Jonas looked at the mark on the wall and shook his head. Elias's enthusiasm for work had never changed in the ten years that he'd known him.

He was seventy and should have retired years ago, but Stockholm City Hospital's Head of Neonatal Intensive Care was showing no signs of slowing down.

Jonas nodded to the chair across from him. 'What have you been up to now, Elias?' he asked.

Elias gave a hearty laugh as he flopped onto the chair. 'What makes you think I've been up to something?'

Elias glanced at the calendar. 'Because it's… Wednesday? And on any weekday, and on some weekends, you're usually up to something within this hospital.'

'Don't ask permission, proceed until apprehended.' Elias smiled, with a wave of his hand.

Jonas put down his pen and leaned forward. This was a favourite quote of Elias's and generally meant trouble.

'I'll ask again,' he said with one eyebrow rising, 'what have you been up to?'

'You've heard of the Kensington Project?' Elias continued without waiting for a reply. 'I put in a request for a doctor from the Royal Kensington Hospital in London to come to Stockholm City to teach us some of her new pioneering techniques in NICU, and I found out earlier today that my request has been successful. I'll be picking Cora Campbell up at the airport in a few days' time.'

Jonas opened his mouth and closed it again, trying to formulate his words carefully. 'What? Who? And no, I've never heard of the Kensington Project—what on earth is it?'

Elias's eyes twinkled. 'An opportunity. That's what it is. An opportunity for us to borrow one of their best—and most published—neonatal experts to come and share her expertise and knowledge with us. What's better, she'll be here right up until Christmas. Can you imagine how much we can learn from her?'

Jonas frowned. 'I have no idea who this woman is. Do we want to learn from her?' He could feel himself getting angry. He was very fond of Elias, but the older he got, the more he meddled.

'Of course, we do!' He winked at Jonas. 'And who knows? Maybe she'll learn something from us. She might even want to do some joint research projects. Now, that *would* be exciting.'

Jonas took a deep breath. As he was Head of Midwifery this new arrival would affect his work schedule for the next seven weeks. He was in charge of the nursing and midwifery staff attached to the NICU. A new doctor might want to teach new techniques. Coming from London, she would be unfamiliar with the standards and guidelines, procedure manuals and cross-check of training that Jonas insisted was adhered to within *his* NICU— because that was how he thought of it.

Jonas was a stickler for regulations and paperwork. Having been burned early on in his career, he wanted to protect both his staff and their patients. He knew just how important that was. Every t was crossed, and every i was dotted. He had high expectations of his staff and they all knew it. Woe betide anyone who fell below his standards.

But Jonas had good reason for feeling as he did. A harsh lesson had made him realise how important rules were, as well as listening to instincts. That was what he'd done years ago when treating a patient in the final stages of labour. She'd been insistent in her birth plan that she did not want a Caesarean section unless there was no other option. Surgery as a teenager had left her feeling traumatised and she didn't want to feel that way again. Having a natural birth would mean she would feel in control and Jonas had been with her all the way. Jonas always promised his patients he would do his absolute best to help them stick to their wishes. But when the condition of her baby had deteriorated rapidly, he'd had to move quickly and follow his instincts, advising her that she needed to undergo a Caesarean section. His instincts had been right. All other professionals had agreed.

But when the woman had been diagnosed with postnatal depression following her delivery and made a complaint that he had let her down, Jonas had been overwhelmed with guilt. His actions had saved the lives of both mother and baby. But he still felt responsible for letting his patient down. His emotions got in the way.

The investigation had shown he'd made the right call. And even though he'd acted on instinct, the hospital policies and his rapid notetaking of all events had saved him. From the first time the baby's heart rate had dipped, Jonas had followed every rule to the letter.

That was why he was now the way he was. Rules, policies and standards protected staff against any complaint—if they followed them to the letter. He also tried to ensure staff weren't ruled by their emotions. He knew how deeply he'd been affected by his own, and had always done his best to stay detached from his patients ever since. He could listen to them, treat them well, and be an utter professional, ensuring a high standard of care, but he couldn't ever let his emotions get in the way.

'You should have discussed this with me first.'

'Maybe.' Elias gave a careless shrug. 'But I've put in a request to the Kensington Project for the last ten years.' He wrinkled his nose and looked thoughtful. 'I'm not quite sure what tipped the balance in our favour this time around.' He smiled again. 'But I did write five thousand words about why I specifically wanted Cora Campbell.'

Jonas groaned. This was always going to be a losing battle. He knew exactly what would happen. Elias would happily entertain Dr Campbell every morning, but by mid-afternoon he'd start to flag and arrange for other people to keep Dr Campbell entertained.

Jonas didn't have time to entertain anyone. His job was busy enough, and one of his senior staff was starting early maternity leave in the next few days due to some complications. They hadn't found a suitable replacement.

'Where is she staying?'

He was asking the question, but Jonas had a creeping sensation that he knew the answer.

'With me, of course!' said Elias. I have

plenty of space and I'll get the opportunity to show her the festive activities of Stockholm.' He rubbed his hands together. 'I'm quite looking forward to it—the opportunity to see our own city through someone else's eyes. I think it will be good for me.'

Suspicions confirmed. Somehow, he'd known that Elias would offer to host the visiting doctor. He'd rambled around his large home on the outskirts of Stockholm for the last few years, ever since his wife had died. Both of Elias's children were married with children of their own, and lived in other parts of Sweden. Jonas knew that Elias was lonely. He was sure it was part of the reason that Elias refused to retire.

Jonas sighed. 'Tell me again, when does she arrive?'

'November the first. I'm picking her up at Arlanda airport at two p.m.'

'Are you bringing her straight to the hospital to show her around, or taking her home first?'

'Oh, taking her home first. Give her some time to settle in, then probably take her out to dinner in one of the restaurants at night. You'll join us, of course?'

Jonas shook his head, an automatic reaction. He wasn't entirely comfortable with the idea of some new doctor coming into his unit to teach them 'new' things. The last thing he wanted to do was make small talk with the woman.

No. He'd rather meet her on his terms, in his professional setting. That way, he could be clear about boundaries, and the fact that anything that happened in the NICU involving any of the nursing or midwifery staff, had to be run past him. There. He felt better already.

'I'd prefer to meet her the next day. When she's had a chance to relax and get her bearings. She'll probably be tired after travelling.'

Elias wagged his fingers at him. 'Excuses, excuses. All work and no play makes you a very dull boy, Jonas. When was the last time you went out for dinner? Threw a party?'

Jonas laughed and leaned back in his chair. 'There are enough people in this hospital already throwing parties without me joining in. Did you see the state of some of the medical and nursing students last week? I sent three of them home.'

Elias tutted. 'Finest days of my life. I love a good party,' he said wistfully.

'I'll meet her the day after,' Jonas said, in the vain hope it might lodge somewhere in Elias's brain.

Elias's page sounded and he glanced down. 'I have a patient. Here.' He pushed forward the pile of papers he'd been carrying. 'Read up on our visiting guest. You might find something interesting. We can talk later.'

Jonas smiled and shook his head as Elias left. He knew exactly what the old scoundrel was up to. Every six months or so, he got it in his head to play matchmaker between Jonas and whoever he thought might be a suitable companion.

Most of his matchmaking attempts had been in vain. Two or three had lasted more than a few dates, maybe even lasting for a couple of months. But Jonas was too involved at work to invest in a relationship and all of the not-quite-right women had grown frustrated and drifted off.

He pushed the papers to the side, instead pulling up the rota for the NICU on his computer.

He wanted to check who would be on duty at the start of November. He trusted his experienced staff to be able to deal with the new doctor in a polite but efficient way. He might have a quiet word in the ear of some of the other physicians. As he glanced to the side, he caught the title of a research paper: *The Basis of Hypothermic Rescue in Twenty-Six-Week-Old Neonates*. Interesting. He was just about to pull it out when he heard a yell.

'Help! Someone, help!'

Jonas was out of his seat in an instant. As he ran out of the door, he could see a nurse kneeling at the site of a collapsed body in the corridor.

No. No. He recognised the familiar shape instantly.

The nurse was relatively newly qualified. 'Good work,' he said quietly as he bent over the body. The nurse had put him into the recovery position, but it was clear it was Elias. Jonas checked his airway, breathing and circulation. He looked up at the nurse, putting a hand on her shaking arm. 'Maja, put out a treble two call.' There was a phone at the end of the corridor and she blinked and then got to her feet and started running.

Jonas stayed leaning over Elias. 'It's okay, Elias. I've got you. Just take some nice, deep breaths for me.'

He noticed the slight sag of one side of Elias's face immediately and his stomach gave a horrible ache.

Moments later there were thudding footsteps next to him, a portable monitor and trolley, along with a sliding sheet. Eight people moved Elias easily onto the trolley and Jonas walked alongside as they headed to the emergency department.

His head was already spinning. He knew

both Elias's son and daughter. He'd make sure he was the one to phone them.

Seven hours later he was still in the hospital sitting by Elias's bedside. Initially, the emergency physician had suspected a stroke, but over the last few hours Elias had gradually regained consciousness and movement in his arm and leg. He was still groggy, his eyes were heavy and his mouth still drooping. His oxygen levels had also dropped slightly.

Elias's son, Axel, burst into the room, much in the way that Elias had burst into Jonas's office earlier. Jonas stood quickly and put his hand on his arm. 'He's okay. It looks as if he's had a transient ischaemic attack. They're going to keep him in and do a few more tests.'

Axel moved straight over to the bed and put his hand on his father's cheek. 'Pappa,' he said softly. 'I'm here.'

Elias's eyes fluttered open and he gave a soft smile, before they closed again.

Axel looked at Jonas. 'He has regained consciousness, but is very sleepy. It's the body's way of letting him heal. They are doing his neuro obs every hour and he's making gradual improvements.'

Axel finally seemed to take a breath. His coat was dotted with snowflakes and was damp in patches. 'Thank you, Jonas. Thank you for staying with him until I got here.'

'Of course. I would never have left him. Now you're here, I'll check and see if his doctor is around to talk to you.'

Axel looked around. He was an engineer by trade but knew his father well. 'What about this place? What about work?'

Jonas shook his head. 'Don't worry about a single thing. I can sort all of that out. If they think he's well enough in a few days, I can help you make arrangements to get him home and see if he needs anything.'

Something flitted across Axel's eyes. 'He was on the phone to me earlier, telling me about some doctor who is coming to stay with him. He was so excited about it. Will you be able to sort some alternative arrangements for that? I don't even know their name.'

'Leave it all to me.' The words came out instantly, even though Jonas was inwardly groaning. Getting cover for their head of NICU would be difficult enough, without the added responsibility of their international guest. Several of the other physicians had extended holidays before they hit the festive period, which was traditionally busy at Christmas. They still had strong staff numbers, but Elias's presence would definitely be missed.

'Thank you so much,' said Axel in obvious relief. He looked at his father with affection. 'I keep telling him he's too old for all this but he won't listen.' His face fell. 'Maybe he will now. I appreciate your help, Jonas.'

Jonas held out his hand. 'Let me know if you need anything.' He pulled a set of keys from his pocket. 'Here are the keys to your dad's house. I wasn't sure if you had a set, so I got them from his office. I'll find that doctor for you.'

The events weighed heavily on Jonas's shoulders as he left. He had complete confidence in the doctors and nurses looking after Elias. He just hoped the situation wouldn't become more serious. Elias was a mentor to him, as well as a verbal sparring partner. He enjoyed his company and respected his work.

As with any hospital, news would spread quickly and Jonas would need to focus his efforts on making his staff feel supported within their working environment.

He collected his jacket from the locker room, pulled his hood over his head and walked out into the falling snow.

CHAPTER TWO

CORA HADN'T SLEPT a wink for more than twenty-four hours. After her initial news she'd dashed off to phone her friend Chloe, a neurologist who worked at the Kensington too. But Chloe had been in a meeting and phoned her back squealing with the news that she too was part of the Kensington Project and was on her way to Kingston in Jamaica.

Both were delighted and numerous calls of varying length happened over the next few days as they both tried to complete their workloads before leaving.

Cora had left lengthy instructions on the care of some of her babies, including follow-up plans if they were ready for discharge in her absence. She was meticulous about her work, and wanted to make sure nothing was left to chance.

There had barely been time to pack her case, and it had been as she was grabbing some jeans and a jumper to travel in that she'd looked down at one of her pairs of colourful shoes and realised they were totally inappropriate for Stockholm's potential snow and ice.

'Too late,' she sighed as she remembered Chris Taylor's words about winter boots. Running on adrenaline, she caught a cab to the airport. By the time she was checked in, she grabbed the latest crime thriller from the airport shop and a glass of wine from the bar, sipping nervously as she waited for her flight to be called.

Elias Johansson was Head of Neonatal Intensive Care at Stockholm City Hospital and had generously offered to pick her up at the airport and to host her for the next seven weeks.

Initially she'd been taken aback by his offer, but after looking him up online, and reading reports about him, then speaking to him briefly on the phone an hour after Chris had told her about Stockholm, she'd known she'd be in safe hands. He was so enthusiastic about her work. He'd read all her research papers and wanted his staff to learn from her. She couldn't help but be flattered by the experienced doctor's praise. By the time her flight was called, Cora was almost jittery with nerves. The flight was bumpy, with turbulence just outside Arlanda airport. It was a short flight, only two and a half hours from London, and she skidded as she walked from the plane to the terminal.

'I must buy boots,' she muttered to herself, wondering if there might be a clothing shop in the airport. She was shivering too, the temperature drop noticeable from the mediocre winter season that had just started in London. What she really wanted right now was a big fur-lined parka, rather than her loose green raincoat.

As she collected her luggage and walked through passport control and customs, she scanned the waiting faces, trying to pick out Elias from the crowd.

That was odd. She'd thought she would recognise his cheerful face. She pulled her phone from her pocket and checked she was getting a signal. Yip, she'd connected, just as her phone operator had promised, but there were no messages.

She looked around. Maybe she should have a coffee. There was a good chance that Elias had been delayed at the hospital. The airport was more than thirty kilometres from Stockholm, so there could be a whole range of reasons for him being late.

'Dr Campbell?'

She jumped at the deep voice, then jumped again as she turned around and was met by the broad chest of a Viking.

'Y-yes,' she stuttered, looking up cautiously.

Okay, so she must be dreaming because this was clearly some kind of romance movie. This guy was too good-looking to be real.

'I'm Jonas Nilsson. I'm afraid I have some bad news.'

Well, that stopped the movie dream in its tracks.

'What do you mean?' She was confused, and, even though it was the middle of the afternoon, tiredness was hitting her in waves. What was it about even the shortest of journeys that could do that to a person? 'Where's Elias? He told me he would meet me here.'

A pained expression shot across the man's eyes. He really was a traditional Viking with bright blond hair and blue eyes. 'Unfortunately, Elias had a TIA a couple of days ago. He's just been discharged from hospital and will take some time to recover.'

'Oh, no.' She was a doctor. She knew instantly what a TIA was, and she was thankful that this man's English was impeccable, because the few words of Swedish she'd learned would be entirely inappropriate.

'Is he going to be okay?'

The man nodded solemnly. She could see the concern in his eyes and darned if it didn't make him even more attractive. 'We hope so.

His son has come to stay with him. But in the meantime, your visit might not be how you intended. Would you consider rearranging?'

She blinked. She'd just travelled from London to Stockholm and was standing in Arlanda airport. Did he honestly expect her to rearrange?

'Who did you say you were again?'

He put his hand on his chest. 'Jonas Nilsson, Head of Midwifery at Stockholm City Hospital. Elias is a colleague of mine.'

She gave a thoughtful nod and looked Jonas in the eye. Head of Midwifery. It was likely that the Viking hunk would hang around the NICU frequently. Right now, she wasn't quite sure how well she could concentrate on work issues with this guy by her side. 'Well, Jonas, I'm assuming that, even though Elias is currently sick, the unit is still functioning at its usual high standard?'

It was a pointed question and she knew it. His response would be telling.

Sure enough, Jonas Nilsson bristled. 'Our neonatal intensive care unit is one of the finest in the country. We have a broad range of highly skilled staff.' Good. She'd annoyed him. She even liked the little spark of anger she'd seen flash across his eyes.

'Perfect,' she interrupted before he could

continue. 'Then I'll do the job that Elias requested. I'll share my skills and train some of your staff in my techniques.'

It seemed that this statement caused an even deeper reaction than the last one.

Which was a pity. Because as he inhaled a deep breath, a waft of his aftershave drifted towards her, like a warm sea breeze. A sea breeze in which any easily distracted female could get lost.

'My staff are already highly trained, extremely conscientious individuals.'

She smiled. 'I'm sure they are. But Elias requested my presence to share my expertise. I didn't come here for a holiday. I came here to work.'

It was a stand-off. And as she was a feisty Highland girl, this wasn't Cora's first rodeo. She'd dealt with more than one guy like this. A guy who seemed to think he could tell her what to do. Not a chance.

Jonas blinked his extraordinarily long eyelashes and had the good grace to remember she was, indeed, a guest.

He reached his long arm over and grabbed her case. 'Let me get you back into Stockholm. It takes around forty-five minutes. And we'll need to sort somewhere for you to stay.'

'Oh.' The word came out before she even

had a chance to think. Of course. Staying with Elias would be out of the question. Jonas gave her a sideways glance as they reached the doors. It was a long walk to the car with very little conversation. Cora had the distinct impression that Jonas already thought of her as a nuisance.

She'd been so excited about coming here, seeing around the unit and training the staff. Getting introduced to a whole new country and city had made the whole project seem even more fabulous. She'd already searched and seen the pictures of Stockholm in the Christmas season. Christmas wasn't her favourite time of year, and she was glad to be away from London and be distracted by a new city. She'd expected the next few weeks to be amazing, but right now her hopes and expectations were sitting like a deflated balloon left behind when the party was over.

Part of the reason she'd dug her heels in so hard when he'd suggested she go back home was that she liked to avoid Christmas at home as much as possible. It brought back too many bad memories. The first, of being the child placed in the foster system two days before Christmas because there was no immediate placement available. No one wanted an extra unknown child at Christmas. It brought back painful memories of sitting in a quiet dormitory with a large decorated Christmas tree. And it was an agonising reminder that she was alone, and essentially unwanted. She had finally been adopted by wonderful parents, but had lost them both years later, so close to Christmas again. This time of year felt almost cursed to her. So the chances of her getting back on a plane and flying home were less than zero.

Jonas had a large four-by-four and he lifted her bright red suitcase into the back easily.

As they moved along the airport roads, she tried her best to fill the silence.

A male midwife. Interesting. And Head of Midwifery at one of the best hospitals in Sweden? No matter how grumpy this guy was, he must be good. Just a pity he was so darn attractive too.

'Can you tell me a bit about the unit?'

His eyes remained fixed on the road. 'We have twenty-five single rooms where families are encouraged to stay with their baby. The layout of all rooms is standardised so staff know exactly where everything is that they will require. Each neonate has their own team to provide consistent care. We have thirty doctors, and one hundred and ninety nurses and midwives. We use a colour-coded system to signify level of acuteness of our babies.' He gave her a sideways glance. 'As you know, Elias is our Head of Neonatal Care. He's responsible for the medical staff in the unit, and I'm in charge of the nurses and midwives.'

Ah…now she understood. When Elias had spoken to her, he'd very much emphasised how it was a team approach to training in NICU— a principle that Cora had always agreed with. There was no point just training doctors in the techniques. In many units there were advanced neonatal practitioners who were often responsible for caring for the sickest neonates. Some of the experienced nurses she'd worked with over the years had more knowledge and skill in their pinkies than some of the doctors.

'I'm really looking forward to meeting the teams. Do you work much in the unit yourself?'

'Usually I'm in there two days a week. I like to make sure staff keep standards high.'

Cora shifted in her seat. Did he mean he spied on his staff?

He kept talking. 'My predecessor line-managed the staff in the unit with no supervision. It created…problems. I decided to be more hands-on. It also gives my senior staff a chance to fulfil their personal development plans and get study days if I'm there to be the supervisor on that shift.'

Ah. That sounded better. Cora nodded her head. 'I've worked with too many staff who miss out on some of the training opportunities they've wanted because units are short and they can't get time off.'

Did she imagine that, or was it a look of approval?

'Can you take me to a hotel somewhere in Stockholm, close to the hospital?'

He gave a nod. 'If you want, I could try and find you accommodation at the hospital. We have rooms for locum staff.'

She shook her head. 'But then I'm taking up a space you might need. As long as there are transport links to and from the hospital, any hotel will be fine.' She gave him a wary smile. 'You might need to let me take a few notes about the transport links before you leave.'

'What kind of place do you like?' he asked. 'Modern, traditional, boutique, luxury, or hidden away? Obviously, the hospital is picking up the bill, so price won't be a problem.'

There was obviously a correct answer to this question but Cora wasn't sure what it might be. She was here for seven weeks. She didn't want to end up in a youth hostel kind of place, or those very trendy places where you basically slept in a capsule that resembled a coffin with lights.

'Somewhere central,' she said promptly. 'I want to take the chance to see some of Stockholm. See the shops, eat in the restaurants. I've heard it's magical at Christmas and I'd like the chance to see some of that. Oh, and a comfortable bed. I definitely need a comfortable bed.'

For the tiniest second Jonas's eyebrow arched, and heat rushed into her cheeks. 'Oh!' She laughed self-consciously. 'I'm just tired. I've been awake for the last twenty-four hours. I was too excited to sleep last night. I keep leaving notes about some of my patients.'

The expression on his face softened. Finally. She'd said something that met with his approval. Thank goodness. She didn't want to spend the next seven weeks tiptoeing around this uptight guy. He was so hard to read. There had barely been a trace of emotion.

They were starting to move through the city now and Cora stared out of the window at the passing buildings and people. Everywhere was covered in a light dusting of snow. It really was a beautiful place.

Most people were wrapped much more warmly than she was. Before she even had a chance to think about the appropriateness of the question it was out of her mouth. 'Can you tell me somewhere I can buy boots and a new jacket? I didn't really have time to get equipped for the cold.'

'You want me to take you shopping?' His voice practically dripped with disdain and all of a sudden Cora was immensely annoyed. She'd had it with this guy. Cora had always been a girl with a tipping point. She could only grin and bear so much, and then her patience left the room and she let rip. Trouble was, the more annoyed she became, the thicker her Scottish accent got, and it was bad enough in London. Last time she'd lost it there, people had looked at her as if she needed subtitles.

She turned towards him. 'No. I don't want you to take me shopping. Just like I don't want to be treated like a major annoyance. Has anyone ever told you that it's time to work on your people skills? I'm truly sorry that Elias is sick, and you obviously feel you've been lumbered with me, but, funnily enough, I'm a fellow professional and I expect a little courtesy. If this is the way you treat all visitors to your unit, I'm surprised you have any visitors at all.'

The car came to an abrupt halt. She was still fuming. But after a few seconds, Cora wondered if he was about to throw her out of the car. He gave her a hard stare with those blue eyes. Finally, he spoke. 'Your hotel,' he said in a low voice, as if she should have known why they'd stopped.

She turned her head to the pavement and saw a uniformed man walking towards her car door. He opened it and spoke in rapid Swedish that went straight over Cora's head. 'Hi.' She smiled. 'Thanks so much.'

The man dropped into English easily. 'Welcome, madam, checking in?'

She glanced over his shoulder. The boutique-style hotel had glass-fronted doors and a dark carpet running over a light wooden floor. A warm glow came from the reception area, and there were a few large pink chairs scattered around, making it look welcoming. 'Yes, please,' said Cora.

'You have bags?'

Cora nodded and the man opened the boot of the car, pulled out her case and turned towards her. He gave her a wide grin and gestured his other elbow to her.

How charming. She threw a glance back at Jonas. 'Appreciate the lift. Sorry to be such a bother to you. But that—' she nodded towards the doorman '—is what I call a welcome.'

She got out of the car and slid her arm into the doorman's. 'Lead the way,' she said with a smile.

Jonas was stunned. By her rudeness. By her abruptness. By the sharpness of her tongue. By the glint in her green eyes. By the way the second he'd seen her at the airport, his breath had caught in the back of his throat. And by the way he'd treated her since he'd met her.

Cora Campbell was more than a little attractive. She was stunning. He'd never met a woman before who literally took his breath away. What was wrong with him? Elias would be ashamed of him. He knew how excited Elias had been about Cora coming here, and he had been annoyed at only finding out at short notice. But that wasn't Cora's fault. She'd travelled from London to a strange country, to be met by someone other than she had expected, only to find out her accommodation was no longer available.

He'd obviously added to the problem with his brusque manner. What was worse, he'd been completely aware he'd been doing it. He used to be a happy-go-lucky kind of guy, but now he was a by-the-book practitioner. He could count on one hand the number of people at Stockholm City Hospital who'd known him in the early days, so everyone now just accepted him for who he was. He knew he was uptight, but with Cora he'd just gone into overdrive. It was clear she was excited to be here, but he had the distinct impression she could wreak havoc on his orderly unit, with her brimming enthusiasm and plans to teach his staff.

But he was also completely conscious of her immediate impact on him. He was distinctly aware that he'd noticed every single thing about her—the few freckles across the bridge of her nose, the way she kept sweeping one piece of hair behind her left ear. The way her accent got thicker the angrier she got—or the more excited she got. Cora Campbell was *way* too attractive. Jonas had spent years keeping his emotions in check. Spending time around her would be difficult. What if his strong attraction to her distracted him from his job? He'd never dated anyone at work—and it was a rule he meant to stick to.

Truth was, if he'd known about her more in advance, he would have probably looked at the rota and scheduled sessions for her when staff would be free to learn and take part. But someone like Cora, with only a few days' notice, at one of their busier times, could cause disruption in a unit where calm and controlled were the order of the day. It looked as if he hadn't done too well with keeping his emotions in check this time, and his anxieties and annoyance had spilled over towards Cora.

He sighed. It was his duty, as a hospital representative, to make it up to her. He looked at the crowded streets. At four p.m. it was already starting to get dark. He knew that Elias had booked a nearby restaurant to take her out to dinner on her arrival—he'd found the details amongst the papers Elias had left at his desk.

It was time to put this right.

The hotel was quite literally a dream and Cora couldn't have been happier as she lay in the middle of the deliciously comfortable, huge bed, wrapped in the snuggly dressing gown that had been on the back of her door.

Although the room wasn't oversized, its quirkiness appealed to her. There was a pink chaise longue under the window that looked out onto the busy streets. Thick curtains framed the window. Her bed was made up in rich white cotton sheets, but the duvet was thick, and a giant red comforter adorned the top of it.

Her suitcase was unpacked. The doorman had been great and given her a map of the surrounding area, a list of Christmas experiences to sample in Stockholm, a handwritten note of shops she might like, and restaurants to try. She couldn't have asked for more.

Well. Yes, she could. A warmer welcome might have been a bit better.

She wiggled her toes. Socks. Another thing to add to her list. Thicker socks. The wind had whistled past on the few short steps into the hotel and her feet were instantly cold. As were her arms in her green raincoat.

She rolled off the bed and moved to the chaise longue, staring at the street outside as she nibbled the plate of complimentary chocolates that the receptionist had given her during her unplanned check-in. It was such a nice touch.

There was a large store in the distance, with a variety of mannequins wearing thick jackets in the window. It might be a good place to start.

She was just contemplating what clothes to put on when there was a knock at her door. Cora frowned, and then brightened; this place had been so welcoming so far, maybe it was complimentary wine!

She opened the door and stared into a familiar broad chest.

Jonas took a step back and held up a large bag. 'Peace offering?'

'What?'

He held the bag out to her again and she reluctantly took it, putting a hand consciously to the top of her dressing gown as she bent down to look inside.

Green. Something green. She pulled out the item and her eyes widened in surprise. It was a thick green parka with a grey fur-edged hood. It took only a few seconds to realise this was a good quality item. It was lightweight, even though it was thick.

'You said you needed a jacket. I guessed your size. Sorry, couldn't do the same for boots, but I can take you to a shop if you want so you can get some for tomorrow.'

He was still standing in the doorway, filling most of the space. For some reason, she was reluctant to invite the man who seemed to exude sex appeal from his very pores into her room, worried about how she might actually react. Jet lag could do weird things to a person. In a flash in her head, she saw herself grabbing him by the jacket and throwing him down on her very comfortable bed.

'Elias had booked a restaurant to take you out to dinner tonight. The reservation still stands and it's only a few minutes' walk from here. I take it you haven't eaten yet?'

She was still holding her hand at the top of the hotel dressing gown, conscious of the fact she only had her underwear on. Her head was still in that other place where he was lying across her bed. She finally found her voice again. 'I was just thinking about it.'

He gave a nod of his head. 'Then why don't I wait for you downstairs and, when you're ready, I'll show you where to buy some boots and tell you a bit about the hospital over dinner?'

Cora swallowed, her throat a little scratchy. Now she'd seen her room, she kind of wanted to spend the rest of the night here in complete comfort, watching the world go by—obviously with room service too.

But Mr Antisocial was apparently making an effort. It seemed her earlier outburst had awakened his hospitable side. Thank goodness.

She took a deep breath and nodded her head. 'Give me five minutes.'

Jonas still wasn't sure about this. He actually wondered if she might just leave him sitting in the reception area for the rest of the night. But ten minutes later, Cora Campbell appeared in a pair of black trousers, a jumper and her new green parka.

Green was definitely her colour. It made her eyes sparkle. And he'd been right about the size. She looked perfect in it.

Cora was chatting to an older woman she'd met in the lift. It seemed that Cora was a people person, and they walked towards him talking like old friends.

He got up from his seat and nodded at the older woman as she left the hotel. 'Ready?' he asked Cora.

She gave a small nod and he could sense her hesitation. 'Thanks for the jacket. You shouldn't have done that. You have to let me pay you back. The doorman had given me a list of shops to try later.'

He shook his head. 'Take it as an apology and a welcome to Stockholm.' He gave a half-smile. 'But don't worry, I'll let you buy your own boots. They can cost the same as a small house.'

Cora's face brightened and as they walked outside she lifted the hood of her jacket. For a second, he was almost sorry he couldn't see her face properly now, but he gave himself a shake and guided her towards a crossing to reach the other side of the square.

As they walked around the edges and past a number of shops, he gave her a running commentary. 'Yes, no, maybe, definitely not, only for tourists, and the best bakery around.' He gave a non-committal shrug as they passed another.

Cora stopped and put her hands on her hips. 'Jonas Nilsson, you gave me the distinct impression earlier that you weren't much of a shopper.'

'I'm not. But I've lived here long enough to know where to go and where to avoid.'

He stopped at a shop with a large front window made of tiny panes of glass. It looked like something from the last century. 'This place is pretty unique if you're looking for a gift. Some carvings. Some glasswork. Paintings the size of the palm of your hand. And some unique jewellery. All done by local artists. Come back when you have some time.'

Cora nodded eagerly at the packed shop. 'I'll come back later in the week,' she murmured. 'It's the kind of place I could get lost in.'

They arrived at the boot shop and Jonas held open the door for her. 'This is the place that Nils, the doorman, recommended to me,' she said as they walked inside.

'I'm glad I'm managing to keep to his standards.' Jonas smiled.

Cora walked over to a wide range of boots and immediately started asking the saleswoman some questions. Jonas was happy to wait. At least she wouldn't fall over on her way to work the next day.

And that was what he kept telling himself

as he watched her try on a few pairs of boots, before finally selecting a grey pair, fur-lined with suitably sturdy soles for walking in the freezing temperatures.

Cora was animated in all she said and did. The saleswoman was laughing and giving advice as they chatted easily. At one point, she nodded in his direction and Jonas felt a flush of embarrassment, wondering what had been said.

Finally, Cora gave him a bright smile before putting her own very flat and brightly coloured shoes in the large box that was meant for the boots and going to the cash register to pay.

She waved her card, then put her bags over her arm and dug her fingers deep in her pockets as they made their way outside.

'We should have got you a hat and gloves too,' he said.

She shook her head. 'I know how much you love shopping, Jonas. I think you've suffered enough for one day. Shall we go to the restaurant you mentioned?'

He took her to the restaurant, which was near the shipyard and had an interesting view of ships both young and old.

He could see her studying the menu. 'Would you like some recommendations?' he asked, knowing that Elias would have relished this kind of chat. It was something he wasn't generally used to. Jonas was perfectly capable of being a charming date if the desire was there, but he wasn't a man normally assigned the role of trying to charm a foreign visitor. He wasn't even entirely sure he could, when he didn't know exactly what Cora's role would be while she was here, and he still had that underlying feeling that she could disrupt the standards in his unit.

He pointed at two items on the menu. 'Depending on how you're feeling after your journey, I'd recommend this one. It's deep-fried smoked pork belly with turnip, chilli mayonnaise, crushed potatoes and sauerkraut. Or there's this one—herring with brown butter, chopped egg, potato salad, and pickled yellow beetroot and hazelnuts. Or, if you're feeling a bit delicate, I'd go for the grilled Arctic char with pine and butter sauce; you could have a side of smoked pumpkin with that if you wished.'

Cora leaned back in her chair and sighed. 'They all sound wonderful, and to be honest I'd like to try all three.' She took a sip of the white wine that she'd ordered. 'I'm here for seven weeks. I guess I'll get to try a bit of everything.'

The waiter appeared and Jonas waited until

she'd ordered the herring, then ordered the pork belly and requested an extra plate. He could let her taste a little. And it was the kind of thing Elias might have done.

It was almost as if she'd read his mind. 'Have you heard any more about how Elias is?'

Jonas gave a nod and sipped his beer. 'I heard from his son this afternoon. Even though he's home, he's still very tired. A TIA for most people is a sign to slow down. He's been running on adrenaline for as long as I've known him. Apparently he was furious that his physician said he couldn't come back to work for at least six weeks—and then promptly fell asleep again.'

Cora drummed her fingers thoughtfully on the table. He could see her thinking. 'What does that mean for the unit, if Elias couldn't come back?'

Jonas gave a wry laugh as his stomach twisted over. 'I can't imagine the unit without Elias at the helm.' He looked out over the water. 'But I guess I'll need to start. None of us are irreplaceable, no matter how much we think we are. And both Elias's son and daughter are married with families of their own. They don't stay in Stockholm any more, and I have a feeling that both will want him to move somewhere closer to them. Although they live apart, they're a very close family. Elias's wife died of cancer more than twenty years ago, and ever since then, his work and his children have been his obsessions.'

Cora drew in a kind of hitched breath. 'Family is what shapes us all,' she said with a tired smile.

Jonas nodded. 'For the last ten years, he's been like family to me too. But I know I have to step back and let his son and daughter be the ones to persuade him it might be time to rethink. If I said it—' he gave a small laugh '—he'd just be angry with me and give me a list of everything that currently needs sorting at work.'

'Can I help with that?'

Jonas drew back in his chair. It had just been a throwaway comment. 'Oh, no, sorry, I didn't mean anything by that. I wasn't trying to hint. I can assure you, the unit is run to impeccably high standards. You won't find anything lacking.'

He could feel his defences automatically coming down.

Cora gave him a look. The kind of look that told him that this woman could read him better than he thought.

'As you've guessed from the accent, I'm from Scotland,' she said, setting her wine glass firmly on the table. 'So, this isn't my first Highland Fling—so to speak. What I'm saying to you is—' she put her hand on her chest '—I'm a doctor. It doesn't matter what I'm here to teach, or to learn. I'm here for seven weeks. I'm not the kind of person to stand on the sidelines and watch, if I can help. In fact, I've *never* been that person. So, if you need help, rotas, supervision, teaching new medical staff the basic procedures in NICU, then use me.' Her fingers closed around the stem of the glass and the corners of her lips turned upwards. 'In fact, be warned: if you don't use me, I might just step in anyway.'

Talk about putting her cards on the table. 'You like to be frank?'

'It should have been my middle name.'

Jonas took a long drink of his beer. The smell of delicious food started wafting towards them.

'I only found out about you a few days ago. I had no idea Elias had asked for a visiting doctor to come to our hospital.'

He could see her taking stock of those words. If she was as good at reading people as he suspected, she would know there was a little resentment in there.

'I only found out a few days ago myself,' she answered in a slightly teasing tone. 'And I'm not a visiting doctor. I'm a specialist neonatologist, practising pioneering techniques.' The words rolled off her tongue and he wasn't sure if she was putting him in his place or taunting him further. No matter.

'It didn't help,' he added, 'that Elias has apparently requested you before through the Kensington Project. More than once, in fact.'

Now that clearly surprised her. Cora tilted her head to one side. The flickering candlelight in the restaurant made her all the more alluring—in a really annoying kind of way.

'I had no idea,' she said curiously. 'My research papers have only been published in the last few years. I mean, neonatology can be a small world. Everyone generally knows what everyone else is doing. I suppose he could have heard through one of my supervising professors.'

Jonas gave a small smile as the waiter approached with the plates. 'I sometimes wondered if the man ever slept.'

She gave a small smile. 'I spoke to him a few times by video chat. He was fun. So interested. Full of questions. I liked him.'

'And he clearly liked you too.'

Cora's eyes lit up at the plate crammed full of food. He took a few moments to slide some of his food onto a side plate and held it out to her. 'You said you wanted all three. Let's start with two.'

He thought she might refuse. Some women would have. But Cora grinned widely. 'Perfect,' she said as she accepted the small plate. 'Now at least I'll have to behave and not stick my fork into someone else's food.'

Jonas raised his eyebrows. 'Is that how things normally are?'

She'd already taken a small forkful of her herring. 'Delicious,' she sighed, then looked at him with laughter in her eyes. 'What, you were never a medical student, sharing a house with people who ate every item of your food anonymously? Or were the junior in a ward area where you're last to the canteen and only get the old withered leftovers?'

Now it was his turn to smile and nod. 'Actually,' he admitted as he started on his pork, 'I was probably the food stealer.'

'I might have known that.' She shook her head, then waved her fork at him. 'You have that look about you. At least I'm…' she gestured to the small plate to her left '…upfront about it.'

She was obviously more relaxed now, but as their meal continued he could see she was clearly tired. It was odd. Sometimes he felt completely at ease around her, then she'd say one small thing, one throwaway comment, about teaching, or training, and he could feel every little hair on the back of his neck stand in protest.

'We should get you back to the hotel,' he said. 'Can you be at the hospital for eight tomorrow morning?'

She nodded. 'That's no problem.'

He raised one eyebrow. 'Just a tip, although the hospital food is fine, you might want to eat breakfast at the hotel. Their coffee is definitely better.'

'Noted. And what about tomorrow? Obviously I thought I was meeting Elias. Will I just meet with you, or is there someone else you want me to meet with?'

Jonas frowned. He hadn't really had time to think about it. 'Let's work on the assumption that our chief executive will want to see you at some point. Tomorrow will likely be introductions to the hospital, and its department and staff.'

'And who will help me with the training schedule?' She took the last sip of her wine. 'I'll need to see a list of the staff disciplines to work out who is most appropriate for what session.'

'No.' The word came out of nowhere.

Cora looked up in surprise. 'What do you mean, no? That's exactly why I'm here.'

Jonas was bristling again. 'I think we should discuss the training elements once you've had your feet on the ground for a few days. Give yourself time to get a feel for Stockholm City Hospital. For the way things run in our NICU. For the staff, patients and parents.'

'You don't want me to upset the apple cart, do you?'

'Excuse me?'

She gave a wave of her hand. 'Sorry, it's a British expression. Probably doesn't translate well.' She folded her arms across her chest. 'Are you averse to change, Jonas? You don't look like a dinosaur. Do you think everything in medicine should stay the same?'

'Of course not,' he said quickly. 'I've been a midwife for fifteen years. There have been changes in practice throughout my career.'

Cora gave a knowing nod. It was maddening. 'Ah, I get it, you're a control freak. It's good to know. At least I know what I'm dealing with.'

She made the words sound so light, so flippant. As the waiter appeared with their coats, she slid her arms into the jacket that he'd bought her earlier.

She tapped the front of it. 'You picked the

right colour. Green for go. That's how I am, and that's how I work. If you want to stop me doing the job that I came here to do, you'll have to be quick. And believe me, I can sprint like no other.'

She patted his arm in a way that made him seem like a child. 'Thanks for dinner. I think it's done both of us good. See you at eight.' Then she raised her eyebrows. 'Or maybe I'll get there before you...'

And before he had a chance to respond, Cora Campbell disappeared out through the doors of the restaurant and into the icy night of Stockholm.

CHAPTER THREE

JONAS HAD BEEN in the hospital since five-thirty a.m., but everything had gone against him. While everything was peaceful in the NICU, the labour suite had gone into full meltdown and, as senior manager on call, he had to assist.

Four midwives had come down with some kind of bug, meaning the staffing level was low. Six women had been in full labour, with another ten being observed. He'd had to pull midwives from other parts of the hospital to assist. Six of the staff on duty were newly qualified, and, having been there himself, he was careful to make sure there was enough supervision to keep them confident in their roles.

He'd already delivered two babies this morning, when he'd been called to assist with another; thankfully, all had gone well.

He snapped off a pair of gloves and washed his hands in the treatment room as Linnea, one of the newly qualified staff, came through, eyes sparkling and cheeks flushed. 'Oh, thank you, Jonas. I am so happy that things worked out.'

He gave a nod of his head. He'd stepped in to help when she'd asked for assistance. She'd been right. The baby's heart rate had started to fall slightly as labour progressed, which usually signified problems with the cord. Jonas had allowed Linnea to continue to be in charge of the delivery, while giving her the monitoring support and professional advice she needed to proceed. The cord had been longer than normal and had been wound around the baby's neck. The obstetrician had been alerted and agreed with the decision to continue as the heart rate drop was minimal during contractions. Linnea had been able to deliver the baby's head and gently slip the cord back over, before a healthy baby boy was finally introduced to the world.

'You did well,' praised Jonas. 'It was a difficult situation. You'll come across this again, and you have to judge each one based on the circumstances presenting.'

She gave him a knowing glance. 'I was tempted to ask you to take over when you appeared.'

He shook his head. 'We're all tempted in these situations, and, believe me, if I'd thought it was necessary, I would have stepped in. But there was no need. You're a good midwife. Congratulations on another delivery.'

He could see the clock on the back wall and his heart skipped a beat. It was nearly ten o'clock. Time had slipped away from him.

Things hadn't exactly gone as she'd expected. Cora had arrived at the hospital at eight. She'd taken Jonas's advice and had breakfast at the hotel, bringing them both takeaway coffees. But Jonas had been nowhere in sight.

Instead, she'd found her own way to NICU and introduced herself to the staff, standing awkwardly for a few moments with her coat. Alice, one of the sisters, had taken pity on her and showed her to the cloakroom to get changed and store her gear in a locker. Once she'd changed out of her boots into her more comfortable flat, bright blue shoes and tied her hair up, she'd been ready to start work.

But there was still no sign of Jonas. This time, Alice had directed one of the interns to take Cora on a tour around the hospital to get her bearings. Unfortunately, Hugo, one of the doctors, found himself entirely too charming for words.

Although he asked questions, it was clear he didn't listen, so he didn't realise just how experienced and senior Cora was. It might have been amusing, if she hadn't been stuck with him for more than an hour.

When Jonas finally appeared, clearly looking harassed, he came up on the tail end of a conversation.

'Twenty-four weeks is usually when babies are considered viable, but some babies at twenty-two and twenty-three weeks have survived here at Stockholm City NICU.'

Jonas ran his hand through his blond hair. She recognised the signs of someone who'd just been wearing a theatre cap.

He gave her a sideways glance. 'You haven't told him, have you?'

Hugo had the continued nerve to keep his haughty demeanour. 'Told me what?'

Jonas gave him a stare, and Cora completely understood why. Hugo's manner and tone were clearly lacking.

She bent around him and sighed. 'I have, actually. Twice. But listening is a skill that needs to be developed.'

'What are you both talking about?'

Cora smiled. 'I'm Cora Campbell, visiting specialist neonatologist. I'm here to teach members of Stockholm City Hospital about new techniques and carry out training.'

'I'll take over.' It was clear Jonas was cross.

'But—' began Hugo.

'*But*,' emphasised Jonas, 'Dr Campbell specialises in early neonates. She doesn't need you to define that for her.'

Hugo straightened his white coat. 'Well, I was only—'

'Go back to the unit, Dr Sper. You and I will talk later.'

Cora waited a few moments as they both watched Hugo strut back down the corridor with his head held high and his hands in his pockets.

'You owe me twice now,' said Cora succinctly.

Jonas turned with puzzled eyes. 'Twice?'

'Actually, make that three.'

His frown deepened. She counted off on her fingers. 'One, you were late. Two, I brought you coffee. Three, you left me with Mr Arrogant and Insufferable for more than an hour. So—' she gave a nod of her head '—Jonas Nilsson, you definitely owe me.'

He turned to face her. 'Okay.' He followed her lead and counted off on his fingers. 'One, I was here from five-thirty a.m., but there's some kind of stomach flu going around in the labour ward and I helped deliver three babies this morning, then I had to go in and assist at a potential emergency section. Three, I can only assume it was Alice who told Hugo to give you the tour?' He shook his head. 'She's had enough of him and I appreciate why. I'll deal with him later. He's not a good fit. Elias would have dealt with him, but that's down to me now.' He took another breath but before she could mention his odd counting he spoke again. 'And two, I concede. Did you keep it? I'll heat it up in the microwave. I would kill for a coffee right now.'

Cora shook her head and gave a knowing smile. 'Sorry, no. I know who to keep happy. I gave it to Alice.'

A smile spread across his face. He knew exactly what she meant. The sister of the unit was a key partner. Cora was right. And he hated that right now.

He leaned against the wall of the corridor they were still standing in. 'How did your tour go?'

She nodded. 'The only place I've not been yet is the labour suite. But that's the last place you'll want to go back to.' She gave him a careful stare. 'But I need to know how to get there if there's an emergency page for a new delivery—a neonate.'

Jonas shook his head. 'You won't need to answer any emergency pages.'

She folded her arms. 'I warned you last night

you'd have to be quick to catch me. I told Alice if she needed shifts covered, I was willing. She gave me a few provisional dates until she checked with you.'

His eyes narrowed. Then he shook his head slowly. He looked half impressed and half annoyed. 'This is my unit. My staff.'

She held up both hands in front of her. 'I know, I know.' She gave him her brightest smile, knowing that he wasn't convinced at all.

One hospital tour later and Jonas still wasn't at all sure about Cora Campbell. She was clearly smart and very sassy. But the underlying suspicions of 'disruptive' seemed to glow like a neon banner above her head.

She was looking him clear in the eye and telling him that, absolutely, it was his unit, and she would follow his rules, but the gleam in her eye made him suspect she had plans entirely of her own.

Although on the outside Stockholm City Hospital appeared calm, on the inside it was chaos. And Jonas appeared to be the only person whose job it was to deal with it.

The stomach bug that had affected the labour ward earlier seemed to be travelling at rapid speed throughout many of the staff groups in the hospital. He was beginning to suspect a nasty strain of norovirus, which was notorious for appearing in the winter months.

It also meant he was eight doctors down, three senior managers, around fifteen nurses and midwives, and many other ancillary services. Each time his page sounded, he cringed, knowing he was being notified of another staff shortage. He was lucky that there didn't seem to be any patients affected as yet.

He strode back to the NICU where Cora was standing with Alice, the sister. 'Alice, we've had multiple notifications of staff sickness. Sounds like norovirus. I'm going to contact Infection Prevention and Control. Let's start taking extra safety precautions in the unit. Last thing we need is any of our babies getting sick.'

Alice didn't need to be told twice. Staff were briefed, safety messages reinforced, and even more hand sanitiser sourced, along with additional protective equipment. She also placed a ban on any additional staff entering the NICU.

Sometimes, some of the junior doctors from other areas would come to observe specific procedures. The sonographers frequently had students, as did the physios.

Jonas had half expected Cora to object. This would thwart her plans to teach over the next few days. But instead of creating a fuss, she disappeared off into one of the offices to go through some of the babies' files.

She appeared a few hours later with a clipboard in her hand. She smiled at Jonas. 'I've made a list. You have a number of pregnancies that are being carefully monitored right now. If any of these women deliver early, I think we should look at some of the techniques I've been using back at the Kensington.'

He glanced over the list, recognising several names. 'You won't have time to train our staff—or get consent from parents to try something new.'

She gave a small shrug. 'The staff won't need to be trained in advance. I'll be here. I can start the procedures, speak to the parents, gain consent, and monitor the babies.'

Alice had walked over to listen to the conversation too. 'Sounds good to me. I've read your research. I liked it.'

'You have?' Cora brightened instantly.

'Of course, I have. Elias spoke about you frequently. I thought I'd better keep up to date on what Pioneer Woman was up to.'

Cora blinked, then her cheeks reddened. 'What?'

Alice laughed. 'That's what he used to call you. He was very impressed by your work. I think he secretly hoped to take part in whatever your next research might be.'

Jonas was stunned. 'He never mentioned you to me.'

The comment was unintentional. And entirely thoughtless. Once it was out of his mouth, he realised exactly how it sounded.

Cora instantly looked wounded, pulling back, her eyes darting in another direction. Alice looked at him reproachfully, as if she were an elderly aunt, and rolled her eyes. Her voice stayed calm. 'Well, he wouldn't, would he? Everything here has to go through our ethics committee and you know how long they take. Elias would only have spoken to you once all those agreements were in place.'

She nudged Cora. 'They turned down an application once because they didn't like the colour of the flowchart.'

Jonas tried to do some damage control. 'Oh, of course, okay. Yes, our ethics committee are strangely unique. They tend to get stuck on some tiny detail instead of looking at the big picture. I'm sure that's why we hadn't discussed you yet.'

Cora gave him a sideways glance as his page sounded again. 'Give me a sec,' he said as he ducked to the phone.

By the time he came back he could see from

the electronic notes that Cora had performed one troubleshooting procedure after another. He watched as she put a central line into one twenty-six-week-old baby, and a tricky feeding tube into a twenty-seven-week-old baby who continued to struggle with its sucking reflex. Before he'd had a chance to speak to her she'd moved on, next to one of the doctors from the unit. It was clear he was having some difficulty re-siting a line in a premature baby. She had gloved, masked and gowned up, and was positioning the baby's arm in another way, demonstrating the angle he should use to get the vein.

She was kind and encouraging, giving clear instructions. There was no bossiness to her tone, but he didn't doubt she would take over if required. Her eyes looked over her mask and met his for a few seconds. It was hard to read her. He couldn't see the expression on the rest of her face. He wasn't quite sure what the message was that she was trying to send.

Half an hour later, line inserted and baby settled, she joined him back at the nurses' station as he replaced the phone. 'Go on then, ask.'

'What?'

'The call you got earlier. It was another doctor off sick, wasn't it?'

He gave her a suspicious look. 'Any more

of this and I'll suspect you had something to do with all this.'

She shook her head and patted her stomach. 'Not me. I'm fit as a flea. Now, do you need me to cover shifts?'

Jonas couldn't help it. He would have to go against his instincts. It was ridiculous to use a visiting doctor to cover regular shifts. It was even more ridiculous to have a visiting doctor who was a research fellow and actually here to teach his staff, cover those shifts.

'Jonas, don't make me beg.'

As quick as a flash, a thought instantly entered his brain. *Go on, then.* Where on earth had that come from?

He gave a half-laugh, which he did his best to disguise as a cough, and shook his head as he stared at the staff rota. 'We need cover on Wednesday night—and on Friday, during the day.'

'Done.'

Simple as that.

She was looking at him with those green eyes, expecting him to say thank you. And, of course, he should. But Cora had a glint in her eye as if she'd just won something, and saying thank you somehow stuck in his throat.

He leaned one elbow on the counter. 'Earlier, you didn't step in and take over. You just talked him through it. Why?'

She gave him an odd look. 'Because he's a good doctor. He just needs to build his confidence. He could do that procedure.'

'But you didn't know that. You'd never seen him do one.'

Cora pulled back and looked at Jonas in surprise. 'You've worked as a hands-on midwife. Trusting your instincts is everything. You must know that.'

His insides clenched. She couldn't possibly know about how that had affected him in the past. One incident had scarred him for life. He'd trusted his instincts, and hated every second, because he'd had to go against a patient's wishes to save her life, and the life of her child. There had been consequences for those actions. She'd complained about him. And even though the complaint hadn't been upheld, Jonas had never forgotten it. He still felt guilty—as if he had let his patient down. It had impacted on him in so many ways. Instincts were good. But rules were better. Rules were what protected staff.

'But you had no idea about his capabilities.' He could feel himself starting to get defensive.

She gave him the most open look and put her hand up to her chest. 'But I know me. I sense if someone is good at their job. Always have. Always will. I would never have let him carry on with the procedure if I'd had the slightest doubt.' Her forehead creased in a small frown as she looked at him. 'This is a teaching hospital, isn't it? All he needed was a hand on his back, literally, along with a whisper in his ear.' She smiled as she said those words, and it struck Jonas that he wasn't entirely happy at the thought of her whispering in some man's ear.

He didn't want her whispering in anyone's ear except his, and it washed over him as if he were some ancient prehistoric man.

He gritted his teeth and pushed his emotions away. This was exactly what he'd wanted to avoid. Cora Campbell was affecting him in ways he didn't like—not at work anyway.

'I would have taken over in a heartbeat had I any worries,' she said steadily, then she gave him a wide smile. 'I'm good at my job, you know. I'm good at lots of things. You just have to learn to trust me.'

For a few moments, neither of them said anything. Jonas was frozen by her gaze and the way she was looking at him as though she could see parts he didn't want her to see. Who was this woman? And why did it feel as if she were getting under his skin?

One of the paediatric nurses walked past and glanced at them both, slowing and tapping Cora on the shoulder. 'Just to let you know, we start our annual Christmas traditions this weekend. You should come along.'

The spell was broken. For a second he saw a wave of momentary panic in her eyes. Curious. She'd just performed a tricky procedure on a tiny baby with the utmost confidence.

'I think I've just agreed to cover some shifts,' she said swiftly.

'No, you haven't. You're free on Saturday night. You can go ice skating at Kungsträdgården Park.' He knew exactly what tradition his colleague was talking about. Even though it was November, it was sort of an inbuilt tradition for the staff here. They all gathered at Kungsträdgården—the King's Garden—ice rink on the first weekend it opened in November. It was almost like the start of the Christmas season for everyone.

She blinked. 'Where?'

The nurse waved her hand. 'It's right in the city centre. You'll have no problem finding it. And if you do, we'll send Jonas to find you.'

This time it was Cora who waved her hand. 'You know, I'm not that great at ice skating. I'll maybe give it a pass this time.'

Jonas lowered his head. He couldn't help the

mischief in his voice. 'Dr Campbell? Something you're not good at? I'll need to see it to believe it.'

She sighed, clearly realising that he had her.

It seemed as though this was a game of tit for tat.

'Fine, I'll go.' But there was something in her eyes. Something he didn't understand.

He put a hand on her shoulder. 'It will be fine, I promise you. We normally meet around six p.m. I'll pick you up at the hotel.'

Then, before she had a chance to find a reason to say no, he left the unit and went to answer another page.

Cora had spent most of the day trying to find a reasonable excuse to back out of ice skating with her new colleagues.

How could she explain to people she'd just met that Christmas was a bit of a black hole for her? She didn't need to do that back home. People knew her. They knew her background and didn't ask questions. When Cora volunteered to work Christmas, most other doctors just accepted the offer gratefully and for that she was thankful. Here, she really didn't want to have those conversations with people she barely knew. Trouble was, from what she'd heard around about her today, this was just the start of Christmas events in Stockholm City Hospital. It seems they celebrated from this weekend, right up until the actual day.

For Cora, it was a bit like being in her own special horror movie.

It hadn't always been like this. Once she'd settled with her adoptive family, Cora used to love Christmas just as much as the next person. She hadn't just loved it. She'd loved it, adored it, revelled in it, and planned a million Christmas activities. But after a clash of terrible luck over a few years, all during the festive season, her Christmas spirit had been well and truly drained dry.

First, her beloved adoptive mum had died unexpectedly on the twenty-third of December after being admitted to hospital with back pain. It didn't matter that Cora was a neonatologist. She still had an overwhelming surge of guilt that she hadn't seen any tiny signs of the aortic aneurysm that had killed her mum in minutes. It was known as the silent killer for a reason. Almost no warning, and, unless detected through a scan, very often deadly.

The following year, her adoptive dad had died after fighting cancer. The light had finally gone out of his eyes on Christmas Eve. Cora knew the true reason that he'd died: he'd lost the will to live after the death of his wife.

So, the time of year that she used to share with the two people she'd loved most—the people who'd completely turned her life around, and given her the reason, will and determination to be a doctor—had been tainted.

Christmas had started to feel like a cruel reminder. Her rational brain told her that was ridiculous. But she was a doctor. She'd seen enough in this lifetime to know that Christmas wasn't a joyful time of year for everyone. Lots of others had painful memories too, and Cora had learned to cope by throwing herself into her work, and by allowing others to enjoy the season the way she'd used to, and giving them the gift of time to spend with their families.

Both of her parents had finally died in the Royal Kensington, so some of her colleagues there knew her circumstances.

Although Cora was usually a positive and encouraging person, this time of year just seemed to cast a shade over her mood. As she pulled her green coat on, and grabbed the snuggly red hat she'd bought in a shop nearby, she tried to push those thoughts from her head. She could put her game face on for a few hours. That was all it would be.

Then she could come back to her hotel room and snuggle up in bed. As she grabbed her gloves, her eyes couldn't help but glance at the square outside. Everyone had been so warm and friendly these last few days at the hospital. Jonas had been there, but not too much. If she hadn't known better, she'd think he was avoiding her, but she'd been too busy at work to pay attention to that little gnawing feeling that he hadn't been around much. Tonight would be different. Tonight, he was picking her up.

Dusk had already fallen and now she could see glistening white lights were everywhere. It really was pretty. The lights were twisted together in a variety of ways, and giant snowflakes were strung between the normal lights. There was a scene in the centre of the square with white reindeer and Santa's sleigh. People were already gathered around it and posing for pictures. All the lights had literally appeared overnight. Last night, there had been none. Then, today?

She pulled the curtains, letting out a wry laugh at herself and her Christmas Grouch behaviour. As much as she'd loved the view from the window of her room, this might be a bit much to see, night after night.

She sighed as she made her way down to the lobby. Again, it was now filled with Christmas trees, and boughs. She fingered the bright pink and purple decorations threaded next to the bright green foliage. Alongside the pink and purple were straw wreaths and small straw goat decorations. How unusual. She'd need to ask someone about those.

Jonas walked through the front door of the reception area, dusting the snow from his uncovered blond hair. Cora saw several of the female staff members take a second look.

She watched them, oddly suspicious as one nudged the other, and they both clearly murmured about Jonas under their breath. Of course other women would look at Jonas. He was tall, handsome, and clearly quite commanding.

But that didn't stop her quickening her steps and giving him a broad smile, along with a loud, 'Hey.' Okay, so he might not have a flashing sign above his head saying *This one's mine*, but she hoped she'd made her point. Taken. Look, but don't touch.

'You ready for this?' His voice had a hint of wariness.

'Of course,' she said without thinking.

'Really?' His brow had the slightest frown. 'I thought you were trying to get out of it earlier.'

She gave a half-shrug. 'Not the greatest lover of the festive season,' she said, not wanting to make up some elaborate lie.

Jonas gave a thoughtful nod. 'Okay.' She

wondered if he would ask more, but he didn't, and that actually helped a little. He held his elbow towards her. 'But you can put up with a bit of ice skating, I presume?'

She nodded and smiled as she slid her arm inside his elbow as they walked outside.

'It's only around a ten-minute walk,' he said. 'The park really is in the heart of the city.' As they dodged around a few people on the crowded street, he gave her a sideways look. 'We celebrate the season pretty hard here— just a word of warning that you'll probably get invited to more events.'

She bit her lip and nodded. He still wasn't asking the personal questions.

'And, as another hint, there is a really good word for the hire skates at the park.'

She looked up at him, half smiling. 'What?'

He laughed. 'I heard it in a Sherlock Holmes movie and always wanted to use it.' He leaned down towards her ear, his warm breath tickling her cheek. 'They're dastardly.'

Now it was Cora's turn to burst out laughing.

But Jonas nodded sincerely. 'I'm telling you. They look like skates, but—' he shook his head '—as soon as you hit the ice you'll realise it's all been some kind of sly scheme.'

'You're not selling this,' Cora admitted as they kept walking.

He shrugged. 'Don't say I didn't warn you.'

'So, if they're that bad, why didn't you bring your own?'

'Yeah, I thought about that, but decided that might be a bit mean.'

Cora laughed. 'For who? Me?'

He was still half laughing as he looked at her again. 'It might be a bit much to invite you skating, leave you in the old hire skates, then bring out my professional skates and strand you in the middle of the rink.'

Now Cora was really laughing. 'Why, Jonas, I didn't know you cared.'

'Don't take it that far,' he said quickly. 'I might hire skates with you, but I still expect you to buy the hot chocolate.'

'There's hot chocolate?' She could almost feel her ears prick up.

'Of course, there is.'

They crossed a busy road and Jonas pointed. 'Look, there's the Royal Palace, and Gamla Stan.'

'Does the King actually stay there?' Cora asked, looking at the immense and beautifully lit building.

'It's his official residence.'

'And what's Gamla Stan?'

'Our old town, and one of our most popular tourist destinations. Cobbled streets and colourful buildings, it's all seventeenth and eighteenth century and is one of the best-preserved medieval city centres in Europe.'

Cora stared in wonder. She immediately planned to come back here some time during the day.

They crossed through the park entrance. The layout was impressive. The park connected the harbour with the main shopping district. There was an elaborate fountain, a stage, a lawn area, and, of course, a large skating rink.

The rink was already busy. 'What's that in the middle?' asked Cora. She pointed at the enormous statue, with iron lions around it, around which the skaters were circling.

'Oh, that's Karl the XIII. He was King of Sweden.'

They walked closer to the rink. There was a barrier surrounding it that was topped with a wooden fence on which people were leaning as they watched others skating. 'What are the tents?' asked Cora.

'They're warming tepees,' said Jonas. 'A place to huddle when you get too cold. That's where you'll find the hot chocolate, the lingonberry or the *glögg*.'

'Okay, you got me. What's that?'

Jonas smiled. 'It's good. *Glögg* is mulled wine. It's sweet, warm and spicy. Just the perfect thing for a winter's night.' He waved as they spotted other members of staff gathered near the skate-hire booth. 'Come on, then.'

As they approached Cora realised most of the staff had brought their own skates. She waited while Jonas hired them both skates, and strapped them to her feet. He was right, of course. They looked distinctly un-skate-like. And as the other staff stepped on the rink and started spinning off in various directions, she realised just what a big sacrifice he'd made on her behalf.

He held out his hand towards her. 'Don't worry, I'll catch you if you fall.'

'The first time, or all the times?' she asked as she grasped his hand and nearly landed flat on her back with her first step on the ice.

He put his other hand at her back and, since her feet seemed frozen in one spot, gave her a gentle push in the right direction.

Cora wobbled immediately and held out her other hand in a desperate attempt to regain her balance. Jonas just laughed and stayed behind her, putting his hands on either side of her hips and almost pushing her along.

At first, Cora couldn't pretend her legs weren't shaking, but after halfway around the

rink, she started to relax a little and leaned back against Jonas.

'Is this okay?' he asked, his voice above her shoulder.

'Is this?' she asked, leaning back a little more. 'You're doing all the work.'

'Just enjoy the view,' he said as they continued around the rink. Other members of staff kept whizzing past them, laughing and shouting and waving.

After a few minutes, several of the girls from the unit came along on either side of Cora and took her hands, pulling her along. She let out a scream, half fear, half laughter as they continued dragging her around the rink. The air was crisp, cold enough to make her want to keep moving, but bearable enough that she wasn't freezing and desperate to get back to the hotel.

She finally collided into the back of another staff member, as the girls decided to stop at one of the tents for refreshments. It seemed to have been pre-planned as she recognised the faces all around her. She'd barely had time to think before something was pressed into her hands. 'I made an executive decision on your behalf,' said Jonas.

She looked down and inhaled. The scent of sweet, warm chocolate filled the air. He handed her a spoon and she tackled the cream on the top first.

'What if I'd decided to opt for the mulled wine, or the lingonberry?' she queried as she savoured the sweet taste on her tongue.

'I figure you'll be back here enough to sample them all. And it was hot chocolate you mentioned first.'

'It was.' She nodded as she took a sip. 'Oh, that's nice. It's different from what I expected. What is it?'

'White hot chocolate. It's their bestseller.' He handed his cup to her. 'But if you want to taste the mulled wine you can try some of mine.'

She gave him a surprised glance. 'So, you *do* share. I'm surprised.'

'What do you mean I do share?' His voice was distinctly puzzled.

She took a step closer, her arm brushing against his. 'I got the general impression that you weren't particularly keen on sharing your NICU with me.'

'Why would I share what's mine?' he shot back, a smile in his eyes.

He knew she was teasing him, and it seemed he would give as good as he got.

'I thought you might make an exception for someone that you'd invited here.'

'Elius did the inviting—without consultation, I might add.'

'But you watched me today. Don't think I didn't notice. I'm an asset to the unit. Particularly when your staff numbers have been hit.'

He gave a slow, thoughtful nod. 'A senior pair of eyes is useful right now. But...' he raised his eyebrows '...you seem like the type that—what's the expression?—if I give you an inch, you'll take a mile.'

'Ouch!' She feigned a wound to her chest as she smiled. Then her expression turned serious. 'I don't want to run out of time to teach your staff what Elias asked me here to teach.'

She watched the tiny twitch at the corner of his blue eyes as she said the name. She got that Jonas was trying to do two jobs right now—be Head of Midwifery and run the NICU in Elias's absence. Maybe holding onto rules and regular practice was his way of ensuring a steadying hand in a time of uncertainty for staff while their regular head was off sick.

She decided to press on. 'I'm here to do a job. Why don't you let me do it? There's a full rota of staff tomorrow. I could start with explaining the science behind hypothermic neural rescue. It's one of my most important pieces of research. I understand that, at first, it can be confusing for staff. One of our natural instincts the second a pre-term baby is born is to get them into a warming cot. If I can get a chance to explain the science, then I can teach and explain the techniques.'

She could swear that right now she could hear him tutting internally.

She gave him her best smile. Boy, Jonas Nilsson was hard work to win around. Part of her was curious enough to want to know why, and the other part of her knew it was absolutely none of her business.

But Cora had always been curious about people and what made them tick. She was open with her close friends. They all knew why she'd become a neonatologist, which was because she'd assisted at her mum's unexpected early labour, and helped to deliver her little sister, Isla. They also all knew she'd then had to intervene when her mum had suffered a postpartum haemorrhage. It had been a scary, terrifying and exhilarating time all at once, and had cemented Cora's career path in her brain. When her parents had died, she'd tried to persuade Isla to come and live with her in London. But Isla had no intention of leaving the Scottish Highlands where she'd grown up, and had insisted on moving to stay with their aunt while finishing school. Now she was attending Edinburgh University, just as Cora had, but was studying physics instead of medicine. The two were still close and spoke every other day. Cora's close friends knew the moments that had impacted on her life, but it wasn't something she'd share with a casual acquaintance. Yet something was plucking at all the curious senses in her brain and making her wonder about Jonas.

She'd only known him a few days. He could be grumpy. He could be funny. He could be cheeky, and he could be deadly serious. She might only be here until just before Christmas, but she had to work well with this guy in order to meet the rigorous demands of the Kensington Project. She had to recognise which buttons she shouldn't push. At times, Jonas appeared like a closed book. At other times, she felt as if there were so many more layers beneath the surface.

As if he were reading her thoughts, he gave a conciliatory nod. 'A teaching session on research and knowledge seems reasonable. As long as there aren't any emergencies in the unit tomorrow.'

'Of course,' she agreed quickly with a nod. She held out her hand towards him.

He looked at her as if she were crazy.

'Shake on it,' she insisted.

'Why? I just told you that you can schedule it.'

She gave a shrug. 'Call me old-fashioned, but I like to shake on things.'

He put his gloved hand in hers and she gripped firmly, looking him straight in the eye. 'See, that's better. I always find it's harder for people to go back on their word, if they've had to look you in the eye and shake on it.'

'I don't go back on my word,' he said, shaking his head at her.

'But I don't know you that well,' she insisted as she finally let go of his hand.

As they dropped hands she raised one eyebrow, then winked. 'Yet,' she added.

CHAPTER FOUR

FOR SOME STRANGE REASON, Jonas had a spring in his step the next morning. He wasn't quite sure why. He was always happy at his work but today felt different.

His footsteps slowed as he realised when the last time was that he'd been this happy at work: the day he'd decided to propose to Kristina—the last time he'd told a woman that he loved her.

That day hadn't been so good. He'd been dating Kristina for a few months. It had been a kind of whirlwind romance. One in which Jonas had finally let his guard down. He'd been guarded with his emotions since the event at work. When he'd finally got up the courage to put his heart on his sleeve and tell Kristina that he loved her, it had seemed like the start of a new life for him.

But things had proved disastrous. He'd gone home early the next day, to collect the ring he'd

had resized, and found a stack of bills in his
post box. The bills were all for his credit cards,
all of them run up to their maximum limits in
the space of a month—the amount of time that
Kristina had been staying with him.

He'd been short and swift with his actions.
The ring had been hidden and he'd had a long
conversation with Kristina when she'd arrived
back at his apartment complete with numerous shopping bags. He'd wanted to give her the
benefit of the doubt. Perhaps she had money
troubles, medical bills, family debt, or some
other reasonable issue that would have meant
she'd had to use all of his credit cards, without permission, at short notice. But, no. Nothing that could excuse her behaviour. There
had been tears, a bit of a tantrum, then she'd
stuffed her belongings into a designer suitcase,
grabbed the new shopping bags and left with a
flurry of colourful language. Her last remark,
a laugh, had been that Jonas was clearly a poor
judge of women, and it had cut deep. A short
conversation with the police had revealed Kristina was known to them for this kind of behaviour, but it hadn't made him feel any less
of a fool.

Wearing his heart on his sleeve, sharing his
history, his vulnerabilities, with a woman he'd
thought he'd fallen in love with, had been a di-

saster. He'd learned the lesson hard. The last three women in his life hadn't stuck around for more than six months. The acute stumbling block of not actually being able to say the 'I love you' words again had proved a major hurdle for any relationship. He wasn't quite sure he ever would again.

Four years on, he tried not to waste any thoughts on Kristina. But something about his mood today had triggered the memories in his brain.

By the time he reached the NICU the spring in his step had disappeared. It was early, but, while everything in the unit seemed to be going smoothly, he was struck by the lack of visible staff. He moved instantly to Alice's side; the sister of the unit was calmly taking a reading from a pump and recording it in the baby's notes.

'What's going on?' he asked in a whispered voice.

'Nothing,' she answered.

'Exactly,' he replied. 'This place is usually a hive of activity. What on earth has happened?'

Alice nodded over her shoulder to the small teaching room in the unit. 'What's happened is, everyone heard about the hypothermic neural rescue research that Cora is presenting this morning. All the babies have had their care delivered, medicines given, recordings taken, and I—as the old girl on duty, am doing the observations while the staff listen in.'

Jonas couldn't hide his horror. 'They can't leave you out here alone while they listen to a presentation.' He could feel his fury building, but Alice could read him like a book.

'Dr Campbell is doing her sessions in twenty-minute bursts. Anyone would think this girl had worked in a NICU before. And you and I both know if I raise my voice above a whisper, I can have every member of staff next to me in less than twenty steps. Anyway—' she held out her hands '—look around. Even though it's seven-thirty a.m., it feels like four in the morning. This place is so peaceful. Isn't it a nice change?' She didn't give him a chance to answer. 'We also have three sets of parents with their babies, and now—' she changed her position so she could point at his chest '—I have you!' She said it as if he were some kind of Christmas gift. 'So, Jonas, you start on that side and I'll do this side. Record all observations and check all pumps. I think Baby Raff might be due for his tube feed.'

She moved off to her side quickly and Jonas spoke a little louder. 'I'm not sure I agreed to this.' He looked over at the training room and, seeing all the rapt faces, had to stop his feet from automatically moving in that direction. He really, really wanted to hear what Cora was saying that was enthralling his usually sceptical staff.

'You didn't,' Alice said over her shoulder with a laugh, 'but you're a good boy, you never let me down.'

He rolled his eyes. Alice was one of the most experienced and most senior of his staff. He sighed and picked up the nearest chart, having a quick check over the twenty-seven-week baby girl who was doing better every day.

It didn't take him long to remember how much he missed working hands-on every day. When he'd stepped in to assist in the labour suite the other day, there hadn't been time to think, let alone enjoy it. Here, things were quieter, and he took time to talk to each of the babies he was monitoring. Gently handling some, feeding another, changing two and saying a few quiet words to the sicker babies while gently stroking their hands.

A little boy, Samuel, was irritable and Jonas took him from his crib and placed him next to his chest and sat down on one of the rockers. He'd just managed to settle him when he caught scent of something light and floral behind him.

'Aw, look at you,' said Cora. 'Now I see the real Jonas.'

He shot her a frown of annoyance. 'I'm a midwife. Of course, I like babies. And when it comes to settling a disturbed preemie, I'm an expert.'

She walked around, gently touched the top of Samuel's head, then moved in front of Jonas, sitting in the seat opposite and scanning Samuel's chart.

When she looked back up, she tilted her head to one side. 'So, tell me, why did you become a midwife?'

He gave an exaggerated eye roll. It was a question he'd been asked time and time again—hardly surprising when only half a per cent of midwives in Sweden were male. He gave her his truthful standard answer. 'I love the idea of bringing new life into the world. Simple as that.'

She leaned forward and put her head on her hand. 'What, no family story of inspiration, or childhood experience of delivering a baby in a field or something?' She said it in a jokey tone but her eyes were staring straight at him.

'Is that what you expect from me?' His tone was a little harsher than he meant.

She sat back. 'It's just an unusual career choice for a young man. I guess I'm interested.

Only half a per cent of midwives in the UK are male.'

'Same in Sweden,' he countered. Then he gave a small shrug, which Samuel didn't appreciate. 'Maybe I just wanted to rush up the ranks in the health service and decided midwifery was the easy route.'

She folded her arms across her chest. 'Not a chance,' she said as she looked at him in interest. 'I've heard the same tales. That in a profession mainly dominated by women, males in nursing, midwifery and mental health all seem to be promoted quicker than females. I don't think for one second that you came into this job to claw your way to the top.'

'Claw? Interesting expression.'

'It is, isn't it?' she agreed. Her gaze narrowed slightly. 'You didn't come and listen to my first session. You were here. I could see you.'

He held out one hand. 'Have you met Alice? Also known as Attila. As soon as she saw me, she put me to work, because apparently all my staff were listening to your research instead of taking care of their charges.'

She leaned back her head and laughed. 'Oh, no, you don't. There's no way you wouldn't have dragged out every single member of staff if you thought for one second that your charges were being neglected.'

'True.' He really was beginning to appreciate just how well Cora seemed to read him. 'Actually, I *was* quite interested. Can I read the notes?'

She grinned from ear to ear. 'Read the notes? Sacrilege. It's never the same as listening to the real-life presentation. You know, where you can look the researcher in the eye, see their passion for their project and ask the questions that dance through your brain as they inspire you.'

He tried to hold in the laugh that was building in his chest, desperately trying not to disturb the little sleeping form against him. He shook his head, and stood up, settling Samuel back in his crib.

He gave an enormous sigh and turned to Cora, who was right by his side. 'I'd hate anyone to think you're short of confidence.'

But Cora was glancing again at Samuel's chart. 'He would have been a good one to try my technique on. There's a note in his chart about birth asphyxia. Who knows how long it will be before his parents know if there is any permanent damage?' Her expression was sad, her voice melancholic.

'Samuel has done well since he's been in the

NICU. He's starting to suck and he's managing without any additional oxygen now.'

Cora nodded, her eyes fixed on the little boy. She looked up. 'But you still won't know for sure until he's much older. Let's try my therapy on the next preterm baby. Let's not wait.'

Every muscle in Jonas's body tensed. But Cora had started talking again. 'You know that research has proved that hypothermia reduces neurological damage in infants who've suffered asphyxia during delivery. The next time you get a baby in the unit that meets the criteria, we'll both speak to the parents, get their consent and start the procedure.'

He didn't have a chance to answer before she'd put both hands on his bare arms. 'Just think, Jonas, we might actually save a baby from damage. Think of what a difference that could make to one tiny life? Isn't it worth a chance? If you've kept up with my research, you'll know we won't be doing any harm. But we could actually change the life course for a child.'

Boy, Cora was right. Watching her talk about the subject she loved with passion and commitment was mesmerising. Every cell in his body wanted to scream yes. He already knew that this had been Elias's intention.

He pressed his lips together for a second,

trying to word things carefully. 'If I can, I'll come to your next few sessions. Once I've heard all your research, *then* I'll make a decision.'

She sucked in a deep breath. He could tell she wanted to argue with him, petition harder for her cause. But something made her take a step back and give a small nod. 'Okay.'

As his pager sounded and he went to move away, she put her hand back on his arm. '*But*, if you don't attend the sessions, if you get called away with work, you'll let me deliver the sessions to you later—after work. So we can still have this conversation later—no excuses.'

He paused for a moment and gave her a brief smile. 'You've clearly been taking lessons from Alice.'

Jonas could tell she was trying really hard not to smile. 'Maybe,' she admitted. 'Again.'

'Do you both just like to join forces against me?'

Cora gave him a soft look and leaned against the nearest wall. 'That's what it is.' She said the words as if she'd just made some kind of amazing discovery.

'What are you talking about?'

'You,' said Cora. 'I'm talking about you. I couldn't quite put my finger on it, but that's it. You always seem to think that people are out to get you.'

'Don't be ridiculous.' He could feel every one of his defences closing like a steel trap.

But Cora wasn't matching his defensive posture—quite the opposite. She was still just smiling at him, staring with those green eyes and giving a little shake of her head. 'You get so defensive. So protective. I get it, I do. But sometimes I feel as if you're constantly looking over your shoulder, waiting for someone to grab you.'

His skin chilled. She had no idea what she was saying, but she was striking every chord in his body. Was he always this obvious? Had the rest of the staff just been more cautious around him?

But if Cora was generally good about reading people, it seemed that her enthusiasm had taken hold. 'Do you ever relax?'

'What do you mean?'

'You always seem on guard. As if you're waiting for something to happen. Don't you ever just kick back and go with the flow?'

Another baby started to make small sounds behind them and Jonas quickly moved next to the crib.

It only took him a few seconds to assess the situation. This little girl, Elsa, had respiratory issues. Most premature babies were vulnerable to infection and this little one had picked up a chest infection soon after delivery.

He moved as the oxygen saturation monitor started to sound. The little girl's colour was slightly dusky as her noises, which resembled mewing now, continued.

Cora turned to the wall and automatically handed him a suction catheter as Jonas lifted the protective shield around the crib and positioned himself at the top of Elsa's head.

Suctioning on premature babies had to be done gently, and with caution, but Jonas had years of expertise. Within a few seconds, he withdrew the catheter as Elsa coughed, pulling it back with a tiny lump of mucus that must have been blocking her airway.

He signalled to one of the NICU nurses. 'Roz, can you speak to one of our physios? See if they can make time to come and assess her again?'

Roz nodded and walked swiftly to the phone, as Jonas changed Elsa's position in the crib for a few minutes, keeping a light hand on her little rasping chest.

Cora thankfully didn't speak again, leaving their previous conversation forgotten. They hadn't even needed to speak about what to do for the baby. Both had read the situation and acted appropriately. There had been no panic, no raising of voices, just two experienced practitioners working together.

He tried to push down the momentary resentment that had flared at her words. She had no idea why he was a stickler for rules. Jonas didn't want any other person on his staff to go through the same experience. Rules and protocols supported staff to practise safely and he firmly believed that.

Just then Mary, one of the physios, walked through the door. She immediately came over to Cora and Jonas. 'You called?'

He nodded. 'Elsa just had an episode where her sats dropped and she had mucus blocking her airway. Can you assess her, please?'

'Of course.' Mary nodded. 'And if she needs it, I can put her on our rounds for chest physio. Leave it with me.' Her eyes drifted to Cora. 'Heard the first session went well. I'll try and get to one of your others if I'm close by. I'm interested in getting involved.'

He could hear the intake of breath from Cora as she smiled and straightened up, immediately launching into her favourite topic of conversation. Jonas, satisfied that Elsa was in safe hands, moved away.

'Don't forget,' came the voice behind him.

'If you get called to other areas, I'll find you later so we can play catch up.'

Heads turned in the unit. There was a rapid exchange of glances and Jonas groaned inwardly. He knew exactly what Cora meant, but it seemed that others were interpreting a whole different meaning in those simple words.

That was the last thing he wanted. People getting ideas about him and the visiting doc.

As he pushed his way through the doors to the open corridor, his tense shoulders relaxed a little. If Elias were here right now, he'd be roaring with laughter.

As Jonas picked up the nearest phone and dialled the number on his pager, he made a mental note to call his friend later.

'It's Jonas,' he said when the phone was answered.

'How soon can you get here?' came the reply.

And all other thoughts were lost.

CHAPTER FIVE

CORA STARED DOWN at the pdf map she'd printed in a few hurried moments at work earlier. It still didn't make sense to her, but then, she'd never really been a map reader. When she'd first arrived in London, the underground had seemed to mock her.

But another week had slipped past, and this was the second staff event she'd been talked into. Maybe they wouldn't notice if she didn't turn up?

'Ready for the Christmas lights tour?' asked Jonas as he walked up alongside her wearing thick boots and a black fur-lined parka.

She glanced up and nodded. 'To be honest, I'm looking forward to getting my bearings in the streets around here. I never seem to know where I am.'

He looked at her, frowned and pointed. 'But you've got a map.'

She laughed and tapped the side of her head.

'I also don't appear to have the part of the brain that was designed for map reading. It's just a skill I've yet to accomplish.'

'Would it help if I give you a hint?'

She sighed. 'If your hint is pointing at the map and doing your best to explain to me in terms a five-year-old should understand how obvious the map is, please don't.'

'Anyone would think you take these things personally. No, I was just going to give you the tip of—' he held up his hand in the air '—following the lights. Believe it or not, that's what most people do.'

He gave her a nudge as she glared at him for stating the obvious, 'Then there's the other hint, that we're starting at the place we were at last week, Kungsträdgården Park.'

She wrinkled her nose. 'Does everything happen there?'

He gave a half-shrug. 'More or less. Gamla Stan really is the heart of the city. Tried the coffee shops and cakes there yet?'

Cora shook her head. 'Like I said, I'm lucky I can walk between the hotel and the hospital. My sense of direction has never been great.'

Once the rest of the hospital staff had gathered around them, there was a consensus that everyone should start by getting something to drink. This time Cora nudged Jonas out of the way. 'Ladies pick,' She smiled. 'And I'm paying.'

She returned moments later with some mulled wine. 'Hope this meets your approval,' she said as she handed it over.

The first sip took her by surprise as the hit of cinnamon, cloves, ginger and alcohol assaulted her senses all at once. 'Well, that certainly reaches places.'

Jonas let out a loud laugh and a few others turned to stare at them in surprise. Heat rushed into Cora's cheeks and she held up her steaming cup. 'First sample of *glögg*.'

She turned back to Jonas. 'I think my eyes actually just watered,' she whispered.

'Novice,' he joked, taking another sip of his.

'Show off,' she muttered as she leaned over her cup and inhaled. She pretended to sway. 'Wow, I think this could make me drunk by inhalation alone.'

He shook his head. 'That's why you're only allowed one. And why we recommend the Christmas Lights Tour. By the time you've walked four kilometres, you'll have forgotten all about the *glögg*.'

'Don't bet on it,' she murmured as the group started to move out into the streets.

They started walking down streets between rows of festooned shops. Above them were gold, green and red garlands. Every now and then they stopped to admire the displays in the shop windows, some intricate, some bold, but it seemed that nowhere in Stockholm hadn't been struck by the Christmas bug. And it was still only November!

There was a large department store, and every window had a different Christmas scene. By the time they'd worked their way along all of the scenes, the *glögg* had been finished.

When they reached a public square, Jonas turned towards her. 'This is the *svampen*—known as the mushroom. You can see it's a popular meeting place.' Cora tilted her head at the strange structure. A mushroom was exactly what it looked like, right in the middle of the square, with several groups of people gathered underneath and chatting together. Next to the mushroom was a huge lit tree. She stared at some of the designer shops surrounding the square, and the names of a few restaurants. 'I take it this is the posh bit?' she asked,

Jonas looked confused.

'The more expensive area—the place where the great and the good come to shop?'

He was smiling broadly as he shook his head. 'You have some strange expressions. Sometimes I can hardly make out a word you are saying.' Now, he nodded. 'But, yes. I get it.

If you want to eat or shop around here, bring your credit card. And make sure you've raised the limit on it.'

He glanced at some of the shops and for the briefest of pauses, Cora thought she saw something odd flit across his eyes. But a few seconds later, he was chatting to one of the nurses from Paediatrics.

They continued along the streets, which were all decorated in turn. Some had hearts in the centre of their strung garlands, others had stars. The lights tour wasn't for the faint-hearted. They had already covered half the route and Cora was very glad she had her comfortable walking boots on. She chatted to two of the staff from the NICU, and two surgical interns that had joined them.

At various points on the tour they stopped. The garlands changed to snowballs in the middle, and then to pinecones, and then frolicking angels. Near the palace were brightly lit royal deer. Cora stopped to admire the palace again. 'It's enormous,' she breathed.

Ana, one of the NICU nurses, nodded. 'I'm a history buff.' She smiled. 'And a bit of a data geek. Built in the thirteenth century, it has one thousand four hundred and thirty rooms. The national library is housed inside, and Parliament House is to the left.'

Cora laughed and put her hand on Ana's arm. 'I love that you know that.'

Ana tapped the side of her head. 'You have no idea the useless general knowledge I have in here.' She gave Cora a nudge and looked in the direction of one of the surgical interns. 'Think he'll like a bit of useless knowledge?'

Cora smiled. 'There's only one way to find out.'

Ana's eyes gleamed. 'True,' she agreed as she moved in that direction.

'What are you up to?' came the deep voice from behind her.

Cora jumped a little, then give him an appreciative smile as she continued to watch Ana. 'I'm playing matchmaker,' she said. 'And I'm just waiting to find out if I'm any good.'

Jonas followed her gaze and sighed. 'Oh, no. Not Rueben.'

Cora turned swiftly. 'What? Is he a chancer?'

'A what?' Jonas looked entirely baffled.

She threw up one hand. 'You know, a guy about town, someone who goes out with lots of women.'

Jonas was clearly holding back laughter again as he shook his head. 'No, he's an easily distracted intern, who needs to study a bit harder. Last thing I want is for him to fall in love and float off somewhere in the midst of his studies.'

'Oh.' Cora was almost disappointed.

Jonas took her by the shoulders and spun her around to where several members of staff had started walking again. 'And you seem to be easily distracted too. Come on, you don't want to get left behind.'

'No, I don't.' She cast another glance over her shoulder to where Rueben and Ana were clearly hitting it off and smiled again.

Jonas was right about one thing. This walk had certainly proved a distraction. The temptation had been high to snuggle up in her room with some chocolate and an old movie. But this was much better. The air might be stinging her cheeks, and she had to keep wiggling her toes, but just being in the company of all the other staff from the hospital, and with Jonas, was lifting her spirits in a way she truly appreciated.

These people didn't need to know about her past and her hang-ups with Christmas. She was just glad that they kept inviting her to all the activities.

'What are you smiling about now?' Jonas had fallen into step alongside her.

She gave him a sideways glance. 'What do you mean?'

'You always have that look about you—as if you're either keeping secrets or plotting something.'

Cora grinned. 'I quite like that description.' She pointed her finger at him. 'Okay, that's exactly the way I want you to think of me, at all times—as if I'm keeping secrets or plotting something. That way, I might get away with more and more.'

He rolled his eyes. 'I'm going to need eyes in the back of my head, aren't I?'

'I thought you already had them.' She pointed again. 'By the way, I tried to find you the other night to go over my research with you.' She blew on her gloved hand. 'But you'd vanished in a puff of smoke. There are three women in the antenatal ward who could go into labour imminently. All three of these babies would be pre-term—around the thirty-six-week mark. All three would fit the criteria for hypothermic neural rescue therapy.'

'You've read the mothers' notes?'

She nodded.

'Which one is your preferred candidate?'

Her eyes widened. 'Why, all three of them.' She kept talking. 'We have the chance to potentially improve the lives of three pre-term babies.'

'They're not born yet,' cut in Jonas.

But it didn't faze Cora in the slightest. 'Of course not, and I hope that all three stay safely inside their mothers for at least another three weeks. But, if they don't, I'd like us to be prepared.' She licked her lips, and caught his blue gaze. 'Most of your staff are prepared. It seems like you are the only sticking point.'

Was she being too direct? Probably. But Cora wasn't going to waste an opportunity. 'We can go over things tonight if you wish.'

For a second she thought he might agree. But, as his shoulders tensed and his back straightened, she knew she'd lost him.

'Let's talk tomorrow. Once we're both back at work.'

She knew it wasn't the time to push. But she really, really wanted to.

Someone handed her a piece of chocolate they'd just bought from one of the market stalls. 'Thanks,' she said, and popped it in her mouth to stop herself pushing him too far.

They moved back through the streets. The early evening crowds were starting to thin a little, but by the time they got back to Kungsträdgården Park and made their way past the skating rink, she noticed the large amount of people crowded around the herd of giant lit reindeer. Phones were flashing constantly as people posed next to the large structures, grinning and laughing.

'Go on, then,' urged Jonas.

Cora shook her head. 'No, not for me.'

He gave her a strange look and she shifted uncomfortably, hoping he wouldn't ask questions she didn't want to answer.

Several other of the staff members ran over and took their photos next to some of the reindeer. But Cora's stomach started to turn over. It was too much. She'd spent a whole night walking and admiring Christmas lights, and, while that had seemed fine, now, being here, back in the park, where everything was so concentrated, it all suddenly seemed claustrophobic.

Her breath was caught somewhere in her throat. Years of pent-up memories rushed up out of nowhere, and suddenly, the only place she wanted to be was back at the hotel and under her bedcovers.

'Cora, what's wrong?' Jonas was crouched down in front of her, his hands on both of her shoulders and staring her in the face. When she tried to breathe in, she caught a whiff of his pine aftershave. Concern was laced all over his face.

But the words just wouldn't come out. She wasn't ready to say them. She didn't know Jonas well enough to confide in him—not when she knew as soon as she started to tell her story, she'd get upset. She shook her head and pulled the hood up on her jacket in an attempt to try and hide part of her face. She didn't want him to see the unexplained tears brimming in her eyes.

Cora took a deep breath. 'Sorry, sudden headache. I'll go back to the hotel.' She was aware her voice was shaking. She tried to spin away, but he caught her.

'Let me help you,' he said.

She paused for a second as he moved his hand from her shoulder and for the briefest of moments his gloved finger touched her cheek.

She froze, not quite sure how to react. She wanted to grab his hand. She wanted to press his gloved hand next to her whole cheek just for a few fleeting seconds of momentary comfort. Although these warm, friendly people were new workmates, none of them really knew her.

She braced herself and blinked back her tears. 'I'm fine,' she said quickly. 'Fine. Just need a few headache tablets.'

'Do you need a pharmacy? I can take you to one?'

She could see the concern in his eyes and for the oddest reason it felt like a hand clasped around her heart. He was being nice to her. He was worried about her. And as much as she wanted comfort, she didn't want this.

She didn't want him to feel sorry for her—and that was exactly what would happen if she broke down right now and told him precisely how Christmas conjured memories she tried to forget and how painful she actually found things.

Now it was her turn to straighten her shoulders. She ignored the way her stomach clenched and pasted a false smile on her face. 'Thanks, Jonas, but I have some back at the hotel. I'm sure a good night's sleep will do me the world of good. See you tomorrow.'

'You'll find your way?'

Boy, this guy was persistent.

'It's not too far. I'm sure I'll remember. I need to find my way at some point.'

It seemed he'd finally conceded. He gave her a nod. 'If you're sure, I'll see you tomorrow.'

He was staring at her with those blue eyes. And for some reason it seemed as if he could see further than he should.

So, Cora did the only thing she could do. She stuck her hands deep in her pockets, turned around and strode away as quickly as she could, ignoring the tears that started to stream down her cheeks.

CHAPTER SIX

HE'D SPENT MOST of last night worrying about her. There had been something in Cora Campbell's eyes. Something infinitely sad. It was almost as if he'd watched her retreating inside herself, even though he knew that was a completely melodramatic thought and he should probably just get over himself.

Over the last few years he'd lost a few members of staff who'd been burnt out by their emotional involvement in the sometimes heartbreaking cases they had to deal with. Hospitals were full of life and death, and the mental well-being of all his staff was a huge part of his responsibility.

Should he be concerned about Cora's mental well-being? She appeared capable and competent at work, but he had no idea what lay beneath.

His page sounded for the labour ward and he hurried down the stairs. Cora met him in the corridor outside Theatre, wearing a blue gown. 'Good. One of our ladies has delivered. Baby is born right on the thirty-six-week mark and meets all the criteria.' She counted off on her fingers, 'Less than six hours old, required prolonged resuscitation at delivery, and shows neonatal encephalopathy in a clinical exam.'

'I haven't had a chance to review the evidence.'

Cora looked him dead in the eye. 'No, but you did have the opportunity. And that's on you. What's on me is that I'm the doctor brought here to train your staff in these techniques. This baby has—' she pulled her watch from the pocket of her scrubs '—five hours and twenty minutes left to start treatment. Do you want us to sit in a corner and wait for you to catch up?'

His jaw clenched. They weren't alone. He wouldn't lose his cool. He kept his professional head firmly in place. "Dr Campbell, these new procedures have to go to our ethics committee and governance forums for agreement.'

'Check your emails. Or, check Elias's emails. Because he did all that before I got here. Your paperwork is done, Jonas. The only person stopping this ground-breaking work starting is you.'

Every hair on his body bristled. He glanced

at the clock on the wall next to him. 'Well, since I do have some time left, let me check. If I find the correct procedures have been followed, and my staff are safe to use these techniques, then I'll allow you to start.'

It was Cora's turn to look mad.

But he didn't wait for her response, he just turned around and headed into the nearest office.

He'd been given emergency access to Elias's emails, but had actually only put an out-of-office message on the account, notifying all people to send their emails on to him. He hadn't gone back through any existing emails on Elias's account—partly because it felt intrusive. But as he scanned backwards he found notifications from both the ethics and governance committees approving of Elias's proposals, along with safety protocols and guidelines for staff to follow. They'd arrived after Elias's collapse, which meant he'd put the applications in on the twenty-ninth of October—the day he'd found out Cora was coming, and just before he'd been taken unwell.

Part of Jonas wanted to be annoyed, but it looked as though Elias had just been laying the groundwork for Cora's visit—which was nothing less than he would expect from Elias. He just wished Elias had told him beforehand.

He printed out the documents, glanced over them to make sure he approved, then sent out emails to appropriate staff with the guidelines and protocols attached, asking them to read, sign and return, and to come back to him with any queries.

He tapped his fingers on the desk, moving to the coffee pot in the corner of the room and pouring himself a cup of the semi-warm liquid. It had only taken fifteen minutes. There were still five hours to start the new treatment with the baby—if the parents agreed.

He took one drink, then dumped the rest of the coffee down the sink before going back to find Cora.

The corridor was empty.

He grabbed the nearest midwife. 'Any idea where Cora, the new doctor, went?'

The midwife was carrying some equipment, obviously meant for one of the labour rooms. She looked momentarily confused, then smiled. 'Oh, the Scottish girl. Very pretty. She's away up to NICU with the new baby. I'm sure she said something about starting a new therapy.'

The papers in Jonas's hands started to crumple. He didn't look at the lifts. He ran straight for the stairs, taking them two at a time until he reached the fourth floor and the NICU.

By the time he was there, he could see Cora in one of the rooms, issuing instructions to the staff.

'What do you think you're doing?'

She looked up, completely unperturbed. All the other heads in the room turned towards him, and most of them *did* look perturbed.

'Outside. Now.'

'In a minute.'

'No, not in a minute. Now, Dr Campbell, or I'll order you out of my unit.'

Her cheeks turned pink and he could see her biting her tongue. She tugged at her scrub top to straighten it as she strode to the door. 'Carry on,' she said over her shoulder.

'*Don't* carry on,' said Jonas. 'Monitor the baby as you always would.'

He waited, letting Cora walk ahead of him. She thrust open both doors of the NICU and strode out into the corridor, turning on him in an instant.

'Don't you ever talk to me like that again.'

'Don't you ever attempt to put my staff in a vulnerable position again in my unit. I told you to wait. You moved, and attempted to start a procedure in *my* unit, without my permission.'

'We're running out of time. *She's* running out of time.' Her hands were on her hips, her words filled with passion.

'The research states the therapy should start in the first six hours after delivery. We are still well within that window.'

'Every minute matters.'

Jonas wasn't going to let this passionate woman beat him into submission. 'Dr Campbell, this is my unit. You don't go ahead without my consent. Have you even spoken to the parents—explained everything they need to know and gained their consent? Because I wasn't gone for long. Did you truly have time to have a conversation with them and explain what you wanted to do?'

He watched rage flicker across her face. 'Are you daring to suggest I haven't gained consent from the parents?'

'Can you show me it?'

'Of course, I can show you it! This isn't my first time at this.'

'Can you show me all the signed protocols and guidelines from every member of staff in the room with you in there? Can you show me your signed protocols and guidelines? I appreciate you've done this before, but not in this hospital. Not under the insurance of this hospital. And in order for you, and the hospital, to be covered, every *single* member of staff in that room involved in the therapy and the aftercare of that child needs to have read and signed the guidelines and protocols, *including you*.' He stepped right up to her. 'My job is to ensure the safety of both patients and staff. I will not allow you to bulldoze in here and put my staff at risk because you don't know how things work here.'

He saw her jaw tense. 'I gained consent a few days ago,' she said through clenched teeth.

'You spoke to the parents without clearing any of this with me?'

'I was giving myself a safety net. I always have this conversation with any woman who is in our antenatal unit if there is a chance they could deliver relatively early. It gives them a chance to ask any questions and take some time to think about it. I recognise that gaining consent after a difficult delivery, and with a very sick baby, can be fraught with difficulty. I only had to go back into Theatre and ask her if I could do what we'd previously discussed. And obviously she said yes.' Cora gave a giant sigh and ran her fingers through her messy hair, pulling it back again and redoing her ponytail. 'I didn't realise you needed staff to sign individual paperwork here.'

'You would have if you'd paid a bit more attention to how the unit works,' he said in a low voice.

The glance she gave him was an indication

she was clearly weighing him up, trying to know when to push, and when to retreat.

'My staff and your patient are left unprotected unless all staff have read, understood and signed all the guidelines and procedures. That is what we do next.'

He didn't leave room for any argument, just moved past Cora and back into the unit. His instructions to his staff were clear. Two staff were to stay with the baby and monitor as normal, reporting any anomalies, while the rest spent the next half-hour reading all the new guidelines, asking Cora questions and then signing to say they knew what they were doing. Every additional staff member who was involved in looking after this baby while the new procedure was being trialled here would be required to do the same thing.

He knew she was agitated. She paced around the unit, planted a smile on her face to answer any staff questions, and wrung her fingers together while she waited for staff to read and sign what they should. When Jonas printed out a set of the papers and set them down in front of her, handing her a pen, she signed without even reading them. He raised his eyebrows.

'I sent the information to Elias. He won't have changed it—just completed it on your own templates.'

'Let's hope he did,' said Jonas with irony. 'Otherwise you have no idea what you just signed.'

He moved away to help a member of staff with another baby. The tension in the unit was palpable. Everyone had heard their spat. Everyone seemed determined not to get involved.

Once Jonas was satisfied everyone had read the protocols and guidelines, had signed, and it was recorded in their personnel files, he gave Cora a nod. 'Now everything is in place, you can get started.'

She almost flew across the unit in her haste to get started. Instructions flowed easily from her mouth. Jonas stood with his arms folded across his chest and watched the scene unfold.

She was direct. There was no ambiguity in any of her directions, and that made her a good teacher. 'Get the cooling blanket in place and monitor baby until the temperature reaches thirty-three degrees centigrade. Start the clock for a seventy-two-hour period. Continual monitoring of heart rate, breathing, blood pressure and temperature, with clinical observations of all extremities recorded every fifteen minutes. Any concerns at all, any readings that change, I'm right here. Talk to me. Use me. We want to do our best for this baby.'

Jonas watched as she put all instructions into

the electronic records, and also set up visible charts around the crib. She'd just finished when both of their emergency pagers went off.

Jonas nodded to one of the other NICU doctors who'd signed all the protocols. 'Are you good here while we answer this?'

He nodded and they both ran down the corridor and back to the labour suite.

The sister met them as they burst through the stairwell entrance. 'You're not going to believe this. We have another.' She looked at Cora. 'You know, the sixteen-year-old girl you spoke to yesterday?'

Cora pulled back a little. 'The girl who presented with no antenatal care?'

The sister nodded. 'She's gone into early labour. Hard. The baby got in trouble with the cord around its neck. Assess for yourself, but I'm sure she'll meet the criteria.'

Jonas knew the sister of the unit well. 'Astrid, has there been a social-work referral?'

She nodded. 'The young mum is adamant she doesn't want to keep this baby. She's been hard to assess. She just turned up yesterday, with what turned out to be Braxton Hicks contractions. We kept her in when we realised her circumstances and that she'd had no antenatal care. Emergency social worker saw her yester-

day. Cora spoke to her yesterday, just as a precaution, in case she delivered early.'

Jonas put his hand on Cora's arm. 'This is a different set of circumstances. How was her state of mind? Did she understand what she was agreeing to?'

Cora nodded. 'She was a sad case yesterday. Very determined that she doesn't want to keep this baby, but close-lipped about everything else. I think she was disappointed she wasn't actually in labour yesterday. Told me she just wants to have this baby, sign the paperwork to give it up and leave.'

She took a deep breath and turned to Jonas. 'I know what you're asking me. Has someone pressured her into this? Is she actually a victim? Can she make reasonable and rational decisions?' She gave a nod of her head. 'She was very clear and articulate. Knew exactly what she wanted. When I asked her about the treatment she agreed immediately, but without any emotion. Just said, if it gives the baby a better chance of being adopted then fine.'

Jonas could hear a million thoughts crowding into his head about this case. 'Okay. She is the mum, and she's consented. We do want to give this baby the best possible start in life, no matter where it ends up. If she meets th criteria, then we'll take her up to NICU a

start the therapy. But I want the duty social worker informed and I want someone to keep a special eye on mum.'

Jonas went to walk down the corridor, then stopped. He put his hand on his chest. 'Does she have issues with men?'

Astrid and Cora looked at each other, frowning. 'I'm not sure,' admitted Cora.

Astrid held up her hands. 'She's only met female staff so far. She hasn't told me she doesn't want to be treated by men.'

Jonas nodded. 'Okay, she knows both of you. Let's tread carefully here, because we don't know the background. Cora, you do the assessment of baby, Astrid, can you witness everything and record it, in case there are issues later?' He gave Cora a nod of his head. 'I'll wait here. If baby's suitable I'll help with the transfer back upstairs.'

He watched as they both made their way through to the delivery suite and picked up the phone to the unit. 'We may need a second team of staff for another baby. Can you start getting our other staff to read the guidelines and protocols? Call in extra if you need them. This could be a busy night.'

One minute she wanted to kill the man with her bare hands, the next he showed the matu-

rity and professionalism of a manager who really understood a pregnant woman's journey.

She was struck by his thoughtfulness, even though she knew she shouldn't be. It only took her a few minutes to assess the newborn baby. She met all three criteria for treatment after her difficult delivery. Cora went to speak to the young mother, conscious that she couldn't let her own deep feelings affect her professional duty.

She'd been in the care system as a child and bounced from foster home to foster home. She'd finally been adopted by a couple who'd never had any children of their own and had a great life. When her adoptive mum had found herself unexpectedly pregnant, Cora had feared the couple wouldn't want her any more. But that hadn't happened at all. Instead, she'd managed to save her mother's life when she'd given birth unexpectedly and then suffered from a placental abruption. The emergency room operator had been cool and calm, giving the panicked fifteen-year-old Cora instructions every step of the way, and the whole event had set her career in process.

Cora couldn't remember her own mother, but had often wondered what set of circumstances had led to her being placed in the care of social services. She knew there could be a multitude of answers. She also knew what life in social care could mean for a child. After bouncing from place to place she'd got lucky with the Campbells, but she still had memories of feeling forgotten, left out and unloved in some of her foster homes. No one had ever been cruel or abusive towards her, but she'd lived her early days with the distinct impression that no one had really wanted her. And that stuck.

So, as she walked into the unit to speak to the young mum, she left all her feelings and memories at the door.

Five minutes later she blinked back tears and left the room. The young woman had been almost cold. Indifferent and uninterested in her new baby, she'd agreed again that her baby could have the therapy and was almost surprised she was being asked again. She was resolute in her decision, and also didn't want to go into her history or answer any other questions.

Cora respected the young woman's right to make a decision and knew she had to accept it.

As she came out of the delivery suite, Jonas was waiting near the crib, already monitoring the newborn little girl.

'She's really quite sick,' he said softly. 'Are we taking her for the treatment?'

Cora nodded as a tear slid down her cheek.

'You okay?' He touched her shoulder and she shook her head.

'Don't mind me, I'm getting old and emotional. Let's get this little one up to NICU where we can take good care of her.'

They readied the portable equipment to escort the little girl. 'What's her name?' asked Jonas.

Cora shook her head. 'She didn't want to give her daughter a name. Said whoever adopts her can choose the name.'

They both looked at each other. It was like a silent acknowledgement. They might have argued a short while ago, but things had to be put to one side right now. This baby was too important. There would be more than enough time to air their views about each other at a later date.

Jonas looked down and stroked the baby's hand. 'We'll pick you a name upstairs, lovely lady.'

Cora blinked back more tears. Today was just hitting her in all the wrong places.

By the time they got back upstairs, Astrid had solved their first problem. 'What a beautiful girl! You look like a Molly to me. What does everyone think of that name?'

There were a few nods, and moments later the temporary name was written on her chart. The next few hours flew past. Astrid had worked wonders and all staff currently in the unit had read and signed everything they needed to in order to be part of the team involved in the care of both babies. Molly's temperature was gradually lowered, and the clock was started.

Time ticked onwards and Cora watched both babies closely. Jonas had no interest in going home. This was a new procedure for his unit and he wanted to be there to support his staff. When the night shift filed in, none of them were surprised to see him near one of the babies. He often spent time in the unit if there were staff shortages, some really sick babies, or some parents who needed extra support.

Cora spent the first thirty minutes briefing all the new staff and getting them signed up. It was after midnight, when both babies were settled, that she finally sat down next to Jonas in one of the dimly lit rooms.

He pushed a box of doughnuts towards her. 'Perfect, I'm famished.' She sighed, then glanced around with her hand poised above the box.

He reached under the counter and pulled out a takeaway coffee.

'Where did you get that?'

He shrugged. 'There's a place nearby that

does food for nightshift workers. I gave one of our porters some money and asked if he could pick us up something.'

Cora looked around, clearly realising that most of the other staff were drinking from the same cups. 'You're really just an old softy, aren't you, Jonas Nilsson?'

He had an elbow on the desk and leaned his head in his hand. 'If you tell anyone that, I might have to stuff you in a cupboard somewhere,' he muttered in a low voice.

She gave a tired grin. 'It sounds like a half-hearted threat, but my brain is too tired to play verbal ping-pong.'

'And my brain is too tired to decipher what you just said to me.'

'Ping-pong. It's another name for table tennis?'

He shook his head and made a signal with his hands. 'You got me. My brain can't make the connection. No matter how much coffee and sugar I've had.'

She blinked. 'I think we've hit the night-shift slump. Let's get up and take a walk around. See if we can get some blood circulating again.'

He nodded and they slowly made their way around the unit, checking out monitoring stations and readings. Jonas nodded over his shoulder. 'Just as well those on the night shift haven't done a day shift too.'

Cora nodded thoughtfully. 'Your staff are good. I trust them.'

He smiled at her. 'So do I. Come on. There are a few on-call rooms just along here. You and I can grab a couple of hours' sleep. The staff will know where to find us if we're needed.'

She hesitated for a moment, looking unsure. 'Look,' he said as he pushed open the doors of NICU and took a few steps down the corridor. 'We're literally thirty steps away.' He pointed to the other door. 'And this one is forty steps away. It's better to lie down here than to have a parent see you sleeping in a chair in the office.'

She groaned. 'True.'

He ducked into the dimly lit kitchen in the corridor and grabbed two bottles of water from the staff fridge. 'Here, take one of these. There's a shower in the on-call room, and there should be fresh scrubs in there too.'

She leaned against the wall of the kitchen and closed her eyes. 'Are you trying to tell me something?'

He shrugged and leaned against the other wall. 'Some people like to shower before they sleep, some people like to shower after they sleep. I don't know your sleeping habits. Boy, you can be prickly sometimes.' The words came out in a jokey, sleepy droll.

She moved, coming shoulder to shoulder with him. 'Taught by the master,' she said ironically.

They stared at each for a few moments in the dim light. He could still see those green eyes staring at him. He wanted to know what she was thinking. What she was feeling right now.

The edges of her lips turned upwards. 'I can't work you out at all,' she whispered.

'Why would you want to?' came his throaty reply.

'Because you challenge me,' she said simply. 'And I think you might be the only friend I have in Sweden right now.' There was a wistfulness in her eyes that he'd only glimpsed before.

'Do you need a friend?' His hand moved automatically up to the side of her face, where he tucked a stray wispy strand of hair behind her ear. She instinctively took a step closer to him.

'Everybody needs a friend,' she murmured.

His own instincts took over, his mouth only inches from hers. He could feel her warm breath on his skin and smell the light floral scent that danced around the edges of her aura. 'It's not nice feeling lonely all the time,' she said.

Her hand slid up to the side of his head, her fingers brushing through his short hair, pulling him forward so his lips were on hers.

Even though they were both tired, it was like a fire igniting some place beneath him. One of his hands wound around her waist, resting just above her bum, while the other moved to the back of her head.

Their kiss deepened. Not a mad, panicked kiss that he'd experienced at moments in his more youthful days, but something deeper, something more sincere.

None of this was normal for Jonas. He'd never dated a colleague before. He'd always just thought it wise not to. But Cora was different. From the moment he'd met her at the airport, she'd burrowed under his skin like some kind of persistent vice. Her confidence, demeanour and attitude both maddened and enthralled him. And the occasional flashes of vulnerability intrigued him. She'd already asked a few personal questions—ones he wasn't sure he would answer. One thing he knew for sure was that there was more to Cora Campbell than met the eye. Trouble was, did he want to push to find out more? She was only here for a matter of weeks. Could he really contemplate a fling with a visiting colleague?

Her hands moved and ran up the front of his scrub top, then she let out a little groan and rested her head against his, separating their lips.

He was surprised at how much that felt like a blow. So he stayed exactly where he was, feeling the rise and fall of her chest against his as they stood together.

As he watched, her lips turned upward again. 'I wondered,' she said with a hint of laughter in her tone.

'Wondered what?' he asked in amusement.

She leaned back. 'Just how good a kisser you would be.'

He was almost too scared to ask, but asked anyway.

She took a step back towards the corridor, her fingers curling around the edge of the doorway. She shivered before tossing a cheeky grin over her shoulder. 'A man of hidden talents. Definitely a ten,' she said as she moved out of his view and seconds later he heard the door of one of the on-call rooms close.

The temptation to follow her straight inside was strong. But she hadn't directly invited him. So he let out a long, slow breath, took a few moments to compose himself, then picked up his bottle of water and walked to the next on-call room, closing the door behind him and automatically flicking the tiny shower on.

What on earth had he just got himself into?

CHAPTER SEVEN

THEY DIDN'T DISCUSS the kiss.

For one whole, painstaking week, they didn't discuss that sweet, passionate, and extremely illuminating kiss—just danced around each other at work, exchanging small glances and smiles.

Jonas was a ten at kissing, of that there was no doubt. The ice Viking had ignited sparks that she'd kind of forgotten existed. Wow.

In fact, things at Stockholm City Hospital were turning out quite well. Both babies who'd had the hypothermia treatment seemed to have fared well. Of course, no one would know for a number of years if it had actually made a difference to their developmental outcomes. But Cora was positive as all the signs looked good.

A third baby had started treatment today and the staff, who had initially been a little nervous, were acting like experts now. They were a good team. Those who hadn't been present at either of the first sessions were all trained and on the rota for the third session to ensure everyone in the NICU got the experience and supervision they required.

Jonas had been around the last few days, helping with the supervision of staff. When he'd told her he was determined to make sure all staff had their questions answered, and would be confident and competent to practice, the man hadn't lied. He was diligent in his duty to his staff.

It was interesting to watch. She could tell that some staff loved his involvement, and a few thought it was a little interfering. But Jonas appeared to read his staff well, knowing who to back away from and who appreciated a glance over their shoulder.

So, if he could read all these staff well, why couldn't he read her?

She was beginning to replay the kiss over and over in her brain. The truth was, she wouldn't mind repeating it. But the even deeper truth was, she wouldn't mind getting to know Jonas a little better too. He intrigued her. It was almost as if he had a whole host of layers to break through before she finally got to the Jonas that lay beneath. Maybe things would have been better if they hadn't met in a workplace setting. He might be an entirely different person away from here.

All around the hospital, people were getting more and more in the festive mood. She was used to it. But Christmas sometimes made her feel as if the walls were closing in around her, especially as those particular dates loomed in the calendar. Even though they were still some weeks away, the twenty-third and the twenty-fourth of December were imprinted on her brain, a time when most people were entirely wrapped up in the chaos of panic buying and searching for that one last crucial element for dinner in the few days before Christmas.

What she badly needed right now was something to distract her from all this. Had she been at home, she'd have retreated to her flat, closed the door and the curtains and taken herself on some kind of sci-fi movie marathon. But being in the hotel was different. The Christmas decorations were beautiful. The maid had also put a small Christmas tree in her room and Cora felt like an old Scrooge when she tried to hide it every night by throwing her jacket or dressing gown over the top of it.

So, today when she was out walking through the older town, she was doing her best to scowl at all the beautifully decorated shop windows. Jonas and many of the other staff had encouraged her to explore Gamla Stan and they'd been entirely right.

The district felt like something from a children's story book. It was packed with cafés, museums, restaurants, tourist shops, galleries. Some of the building fronts were painted in vivid shades of red, yellow and green. Coupled with a dusting of snow and cobblestone streets, Cora half expected a witch on a broomstick to fly overhead, next to reindeer pulling a sleigh.

She lost several hours in the shops, buying some woodwork, jewellery, and then finding a sci-fi book shop with some very tempting board games. Wonderful smells continued to drift around her and it wasn't long before her stomach started to rumble.

She was peering in the window of one of the bakeries when she felt a tap on her shoulder. 'I'd recognise that green coat anywhere,' said the accented voice.

Her stomach leapt and she turned around to see Jonas holding a paper bag with a giant loaf inside. 'What are you doing here?' she asked.

He raised his eyebrows and lifted the loaf. 'I'm on a retrieval mission for the theatre team. I told them that when I came in at two p.m. today, I'd bring some bread for them.'

'You're working today?' He nodded. 'One of

the other managers needs a few hours off this afternoon. Her daughter is in a play at school.'

Those few words made Cora's heart swell. Jonas really was a good guy. 'What's the other bag?' she asked.

His face fell a little. 'It's Elias's favourite apricot pastries. I'll run them over to him later today.'

She nodded, then looked around and held up her hands, which were weighed down with bags. 'Okay, I've been shopping all morning and am looking for somewhere to go for a coffee and some cakes. Where do you recommend? They all look good around here.'

He nodded. 'Come along, I'll show you. Is it definitely cake you want, or something more substantial?'

'Oh, no, it's cake. Can you smell this place? I might just eat all the cakes. There's no way I can be here and resist eating cake.'

They walked along the street together, and when they were almost at the castle, Jonas nudged her, and pointed towards a cute-looking café. She spun around. 'Will you join me?' she asked. 'Or don't you have enough time?'

There was a large clock visible where they were standing and it was only eleven. But she had no idea what other plans he had for the day.

Jonas nodded solemnly and smiled. 'I think

it's my duty to introduce you to all the cakes that Stockholm has to offer.'

He pushed open the door to the café and joined her at a table near the window. He glanced over at the glass-fronted cabinet. 'So, what's it to be? Scrumptious croissants, cinnamon buns, fruit and nut loaf, or blueberry and raspberry pie?'

'I swear I'm putting on ten pounds every time I inhale around here,' said Cora, watching as a waitress walked past with delicious-looking items on her tray. 'I want what they're having,' she said as the plates and mugs were slid onto the table.

'Well, that's easy, then.' Jonas said a few words to the smiling waitress as she passed by. She nodded and disappeared.

Cora gestured down at her bags. 'You didn't tell me how addictive this place is. Don't leave me unsupervised again. I'll likely buy everything and eat everything.'

She was smiling but Jonas's brow creased for a few moments. Didn't he know she was joking?

He looked down at the numerous bags she had sitting on the floor, the crease in his brow deepening as he stared.

Then he blinked and his pale blue eyes rested on her again.

'I'm sure that won't happen,' he said softly.

She unzipped her jacket, feeling instantly flustered. Cora had the distinct impression that she was missing something here.

The waitress appeared and put two delicious-smelling white hot chocolates on their table along with two portions of warm blueberry and raspberry pie complete with ice cream. 'Wow, ice cream in the middle of winter. I wouldn't have believed it if I hadn't seen it for myself.'

She wasn't quite sure what was on Jonas's mind, but she was determined to lift the mood. They'd kissed just over a week ago now, and neither of them had talked about it since.

As he took his first spoonful of pie, she decided to throw caution to the wind. 'So, tell me, do you kiss every visiting doctor that comes to Stockholm City Hospital?'

His eyes widened and he started to choke on his pie. Several other customers turned to look and Cora had to jump up and give him a couple of claps on the back before he finally stopped. The waitress appeared with a glass of water and Cora sat back down in time to see Jonas wipe the tears that were streaming down his face.

'Are you okay?' asked the waitress.

He nodded. 'Fine. Sorry. It just went down the wrong way.'

She nodded, waiting a few moments before leaving.

Cora picked up her own spoon, now feeling badly instead of bold.

'Maybe a question for another time?'

Jonas shook his head and took a drink of the water. 'No. It's not. And no, I don't kiss every visiting doctor. You're the only one.'

She leaned her head on one hand. 'Ahh, so I'm special, then?' She wanted to joke, she wanted to flirt. She was still surrounded by all things Christmas and she wanted her mind to be someplace else.

He raised one eyebrow. 'Maybe.'

She grinned at him. 'You playing hard to get?'

His brow creased again and she waved her hand. 'Don't worry, it's an expression that probably doesn't translate well.'

He stirred his hot chocolate. It was clear he was thinking about something. 'Are you going to the Lucia procession?'

Now it was her turn to frown and shake her head. 'What's that?'

'It's next week. There are many processions of Lucia and they all take place in December. A young girl is asked to act as lady of light, or

Lucia, as we call her. She wears a white costume and has candles on her head, and there is usually a singing procession following her. There's always one in Stockholm and most of the hospital staff attend.' He paused for a second, then added, 'Or there's the night out beside the world's largest Christmas tree—you'll have seen it already at Gamla Stan. Or there's the living Christmas advent calendar. You might have seen it already. Every night, a window somewhere in Gamla Stan will open at six-fifteen p.m.—on Christmas Eve it opens at eleven-thirty a.m.—and one or more heads will pop out—an actor, a singer, a storyteller—and offer fifteen minutes of Christmas advent delight. If you look out for banners hung from windows that say *Här öppnar luckan*, you'll know where the surprise window will be that night.'

He was clearly waiting for a response, but, after flirting with him, Cora was finding it hard to say the word she wanted to: no.

She licked her lips and tried to find something appropriate to say. 'Is everything about Christmas? Isn't there anything that's just about Stockholm?'

She could sense his eyes on her for a few moments of consideration.

'Don't you like Christmas, Cora?' He asked

the question in a gentle way that made her re-alise he already knew the answer. He was just giving her a chance to say what she wanted.

She bit her lip and met his gaze. 'I find it a bit tough. Family reasons. I want to be socia-ble with the rest of the staff—I do. But every single thing we do is about Christmas. I don't want to appear like a Scrooge because I don't love it quite as much as others.'

He reached over and squeezed her hand. 'You're right. Most of the trips this time of year are about Christmas. We can find something different to do. A visit to the Vasa Museum perhaps? Or we could do a boat trip—this city stretches across fourteen islands. You've only seen a few.'

She nodded gratefully as he kept talking.

'Maybe, though, if you don't have good memories of Christmas, it might be nice to create some new ones? And Stockholm is new to you—perhaps you could create some new memories here?'

Her skin prickled. He was being sincere, and it made her feel stripped back and bare. As if all her past experiences and fears were ex-posed. Her involuntary action was the same as always—to brush things off.

'Can I take that under advisement?'

Jonas looked puzzled again and she waved her hand. 'Just another turn of phrase. Ignore me.'

There was silence for a few moments as they both ate. The door to the café opened again, letting in a fierce gust of cold air, and another couple walked in hand in hand. Something twisted inside Cora.

She couldn't ever remember looking like that. So in love, so caught up in the moment that nothing else mattered. She tried not to stare as they stood at the counter together selecting cakes, then sloping off to one of the booths near the back of the café.

When she looked up she realised Jonas was watching them too. He shrugged. 'Oh, to be young.'

There was something melancholy about his throwaway words. And she was suddenly struck by the fact that for the last few minutes she'd been immersed in herself and not thinking about Jonas. She knew there was a story hidden deep down somewhere. It was in everything he said, everything he did, and the way he reacted to things. His need for process drove her crazy. But she'd seen how well he connected with patients. Part of her wondered if being in management was the right thing for Jonas. Management came with its own challenges—one of which was that it often took an excellent hands-on member of staff further away from the patients.

She glanced back at the younger couple. 'They're not so young,' she said, squinting a little to get a better look. 'Mid-twenties?'

Jonas nodded in agreement. 'Maybe.' There was still something wistful in his tone. She wanted to prod. She wanted to ask questions but wasn't quite sure how he might respond. Did kissing someone give her the right to dig deeper?

'You haven't mentioned family much—do you have family in Stockholm?'

He shook his head. 'My family stay in Sundsvall. It's about a four-hour drive. I moved to Stockholm to train to be a nurse and midwife and found that I liked it here. I've been here since I was eighteen.'

'Do you ever go back home?'

'Sometimes I visit my parents and my sister in holidays.'

'Are you going home for Christmas?'

He shook his head. 'I usually volunteer to work so other managers who have families can have the time off. I hope that when my time comes, someone will do the same for me.'

She was pretty sure her stomach was fluttering right now, and it wasn't the raspberry pie. 'You plan to settle down sometime?'

He leaned back in his chair. 'Some day. Doesn't everyone?' His eyes fixed on hers.

Cora hesitated. 'I sometimes wonder if I'm the settling-down type.'

His gaze was steady. 'Well, only you can decide that. I guess it just depends what priorities you have in your life. And timing, of course.'

'You haven't met anyone you wanted to settle down with?' As she asked the question she noticed him shift uncomfortably and she cringed. Please don't let there be some dead wife in the background and she'd just monumentally put her foot in it.

His gaze was now fixed on the window to the street outside. Surely if there had been something, or someone, significant in his past, one of the other staff might have mentioned it? But then, the staff were loyal to Jonas. Would they really tell a temporary newcomer something private or personal about their boss? Probably not. Maybe she should tread a little more carefully.

'Not yet,' he said finally. She could almost see something turn on in his eyes—as if he'd never really given it much thought before, but now...now it was something he might consider. 'I guess I've just not been lucky.' He took a sip of his hot chocolate. 'Not met the right woman yet.'

She could swear there was something glittering in the air between them. So much unsaid. Her brain was screaming *How about me?* And, maybe she was crazy, but as he looked at her the corners of his mouth edged upwards, as if he were having the same thoughts as she was. When he spoke again, his voice was low. 'What about you? No Mr Right tucked away somewhere?'

She shook her head and laughed. 'Plenty of Mr Wrongs, Mr Never-Could-Be-Rights, and Mr Absolute Disasters, though. I tend to get too caught up in work to pay much attention to whoever I'm dating. I think I'm probably the worst girlfriend in the world.'

He held up his hot chocolate. 'I'll drink to that.'

She laughed and held up hers. 'What—are you the worst boyfriend too?'

'Oh, no, but I'm happy to drink to you being the worst girlfriend.'

'Cheeky!' She clunked her mug against his and ate some more of her pie. 'You said you're going to meet Elias. Do you think I might get to meet him in person at some point, before I leave?'

He wrinkled his nose. 'What—you have another, nearly three weeks? I'll see how he is today. Elias is a proud man. He wouldn't want to meet you unless he was at a stage where he could converse properly with you.'

'He's not there yet?'

'Maybe. He's improving all the time. I saw him again last week, and he was able to walk with a stick. He was still stumbling with some words, and his thought processes were a little delayed. Let me ask him when I visit later today. I'll let you know what he says.'

'Will you tell him about the babies?'

There was the briefest hesitation. 'Of course, I will. He'll want to know all about it.'

'And you'll tell him it's been a success?' she pushed.

'I'll tell him the procedures went well, and our staff training and monitoring systems are in place. I can't tell him it was a success as we don't know yet that it is a success. We won't know the outcomes for these babies for a few years.' This time it was him who was pushing.

'But the immediate outcomes were evident.'

He nodded slowly. 'Yes, but we have to view these things in context.'

Cora sat back with a sigh and shook her head. 'You don't want this to succeed, do you? You're so against change that no matter how well this works, you just won't let it continue.' Frustration was building inside her. She'd thought they'd made strides towards this being an implementable procedure at Stockholm City Hospital. A step forward for babies affected by hypoxic ischaemic encephalopathy. But every time she thought they'd made some headway, they seemed to jump backwards instead.

Jonas looked at her with an incredulous expression. 'Where on earth did you get that from? I'm just asking you to have a bit of context around the work so far and not to jump too far ahead. We've used the treatment on three babies, Cora. *Three*. Since when did that become a number that makes this treatment the one to use? You've been involved in research studies. You know that's not how this works. And we won't know the true outcomes for these babies for years.'

She leaned forward, pressing both her hands on the table. 'But this is *not* a research study. This is fact. The studies have been done. I'm here to teach, not to tiptoe around every person and constantly ask permission to breathe!'

Her heart was racing in her chest and her voice had become a bit louder, causing people to turn around and look at them, with a few raised eyebrows.

But Jonas wasn't ready to back down. He leaned back across the table to her. His voice was low, and hissing. 'But your research was done in the UK. A different population. A different demographic. A different healthcare and social care system. Things aren't automatically translatable. I shouldn't have to tell you that.'

Cora stood up sharply, her chair tilting back dangerously. 'You're impossible.'

Jonas leaned back in his chair. While she was boiling mad, he looked completely unperturbed. It was as if he was baiting her.

'And you're irrational.'

It was like someone jabbing a red-hot poker into her side. How dared he call her irrational? She was so mad she couldn't speak—not that he deserved a response.

She slid her arms into her jacket, bent down and snatched up her shopping bags, fumbling to fit them all in her hands before turning and storming out of the door.

The freezing-cold air did nothing to cool her temper. She stomped down the street without a backwards glance, determined to get as far away as possible from Mr Ice Viking.

She had a job to do. And he wouldn't get in her way. She wouldn't let him.

CHAPTER EIGHT

Two days later and she hadn't set eyes on him.

Cora was the ultimate professional. In the NICU she was all smiles. She'd written a few more protocols for the procedure and asked Alice for advice on how to put them through all the relevant committees.

Alice had waved her hand. 'Jonas will do all that for you,' she'd said casually.

'I like to see things through myself,' she'd insisted. 'Plus, I like to find out all the procedures anywhere that I'm working. Each hospital works differently, and it's good for me to get a handle on different operating procedures.'

If Alice had been suspicious, she hadn't said so, just scribbled down some names and numbers of people for Cora to get in touch with.

Forty minutes later when there had been a page from the antenatal ward that another of their patients had gone into early labour, she'd decided to go on down.

Her phone buzzed as she ran down the stairs. It was Chloe. They'd been ping-ponging messages to each other after Cora had raged about Jonas a few days ago.

Just thinking. Can't remember the last time you ranted about someone quite so much. If you ask me, there's more to this than a disagreement about work. Exactly how attractive is Jonas Nilsson?

Cora's mouth bounced open. Chloe was too smart for her own good.

Viking-like. But far too arrogant for me to care how attractive he is.

Dots appeared. Chloe was immediately typing a response.

You've kissed him, haven't you?

Cora actually stopped mid-step.

Why on earth would you say that??????????

She was shaking her head as Chloe typed back.

Knew it.

She let out a sigh and put her phone back in her pocket. Chloe could always read her like a book.

As she reached the labour suite, there was that eerie kind of calm. There was no sign of any staff, and the corridor was silent—never a good sign in a labour ward.

She made her way along the corridor, towards the emergency theatre at the end. Just as she reached the swing doors, a midwife burst through them, wearing a blood-stained plastic apron. She gave Cora a quick glance up and down before a flicker of recognition crossed her face and she pointed a gloved hand. 'NICU doctor?'

Cora nodded without speaking.

'Good, with me. Emergency.' The midwife gave a sharp nod of her head and pushed open the doors.

Cora could tell immediately that this was where the majority of the staff were. Someone was lying on the floor, and it took her a few moments to realise it was a fellow doctor, who was pregnant. She went immediately to assist, but a voice from the theatre table stopped her.

'No, leave her. We need you here.'

Cora's head flicked from one place to the

other. Every instinct in her wanted to help her fellow colleague on the theatre floor, but there were three members of staff already around her. One of them caught her eye. 'She's diabetic. Had a hypoglycaemic attack. We can deal with this.'

Cora didn't recognise the obstetrician in the cap and mask at the theatre table, but there were twelve at Stockholm City Hospital and she hadn't met them all.

His voice was deep. 'I need a neonatologist. This baby will need resuscitated.' He was already cutting through the woman's abdomen.

Cora stepped to the sinks and gave her hands a quick wash. Turning around, she found a theatre nurse with a gown ready for her to step into, and another with a pair of waiting gloves, and a third placed a cap on her head.

She recognised one of the NICU nurses waiting next to the neonatal crib. She thrust her hands into the gloves, just as the obstetrician lifted out the silent baby.

As Cora took the baby, her motions became automatic. She'd unfortunately done this on many occasions. A voice she recognised was at her side and she looked up to see Jonas appear and tie a mask around her face. Some babies needed encouragement to breathe after delivery, but Cora knew nothing about the circumstances of this case, and this little one looked a little too flat for her liking.

She spoke clearly to the NICU nurse, who was just as well versed in this as she was, assessing airway, breathing and circulation. Jonas handed her a suction tube, as she tried to stimulate the baby to breathe.

Nothing. There was a noise behind them and she turned her head in time to see her colleague on the floor thrash out with her arms and legs. It was clear she was confused. Hypoglycaemic attacks frequently did that, and it could be a few minutes before things calmed down. In an ideal situation they would have taken her somewhere else, but for the next few minutes, the floor was probably the safest place for her.

Cora continued her assessment of the baby as Jonas systematically connected her to all the monitoring equipment. It was a little girl and her colour was extremely poor. Her pulse was weak but rapid and thready, and there was no respiratory effort at all, even with a bag and mask. After another few moments she nodded to Jonas. 'I'm going to intubate.'

She moved to the head of the crib and Jonas automatically put everything she needed into her hands. Airways could be tricky, particularly in small pre-term babies, but Cora slid the tube in with no problem and started the procedures to connect the little girl to the machinery.

Now it was Cora's turn to hold her breath, until the little girl's skin finally started to lose the dusky tone and pink up.

She spent the next few moments inserting a line. Premedication was usually given prior to intubation in the neonatal unit, but wasn't appropriate for intubations in the delivery suite. Cora wanted to ensure that now an airway was established she could do her utmost to ensure this little girl was given the medications that would assist her.

Cora finally lifted her head to look at the obstetrician while another nurse put an ID bracelet on the baby. 'I'm going to take this little one up to NICU.'

As another alarm sounded, this time for the mother, the obstetrician nodded. 'Thanks for your assistance. Jonas said you would step in.'

She exchanged glances for the briefest of seconds with Jonas, and then the two of them started to push the crib and ventilator out to the lift. Their doctor colleague was now in a sitting position on the floor and drinking some orange juice.

Once they were clear of the theatre, Cora

pressed the button for the lift and looked at Jonas. 'What on earth happened in there?'

He frowned tightly. 'Everything. Eve passed out. One minute she was there and talking, the next she was on the floor. I had already paged you about the delivery and knew you were likely on your way down. Just as well, as at that point they lost the baby's heartbeat.'

Cora shuddered. Her eyes on her little patient. 'As soon as I walked into the labour suite I knew something was wrong.'

'Chaos?'

'The opposite. Not a single person and complete silence.'

Jonas closed his eyes for a second. 'Never a good sign.'

'Nope.' She touched the cheek of the little girl. 'Do we know a name?'

He nodded. 'Her mother told me before we got to Theatre that she intended to call her Rose.'

'You were already down there?'

He nodded again. 'Yes. There had been some issues on the antenatal ward, and the labour suite today.'

'What?' The question came out automatically, and as soon as she noticed the dark expression on his face, she wished she hadn't asked.

'Two staff were involved in a car accident this morning. One worked in each area. Both are serious, and are in general theatres, right now.'

'Oh, no.'

He inhaled deeply. 'I had to send some staff home, and I had to phone the families.'

She reached her hand over and touched his. 'That must have been hard.'

'That's the job. I've called extra staff in, and another manager.'

'And what about that doctor? I've never met her before.'

'The neonatologist? Eve has been off during her pregnancy. She's a Type One diabetic and had been having frequent hypos. She literally came back to work two hours ago.'

'Poor soul. She'll need to go off again. Will someone check her over?'

'I'll make sure of it.' He glanced at Cora. 'It's a shame. You would have liked working with her. She's a great doctor.'

As the lift doors pinged open, two of the NICU staff were waiting for them and grabbed one end of the crib and the portable ventilator.

They rolled smoothly into the NICU and spent the next half-hour getting baby Rose set up in the unit. Jonas disappeared while Cora spent some time with the frazzled dad who appeared upstairs, explaining exactly what was happening with his newly born daughter.

By the time Jonas reappeared with two ham bagels in his hand, Cora didn't even realise that four hours had passed since she'd first received the page.

As he sat down next to her in the office, and wordlessly handed her a bagel, Cora took a deep breath. 'Wow.'

He took a bite of his bagel and a few moments later gave an agreed, 'Wow.'

'Is Eve okay?'

He smiled. 'Angry, embarrassed, annoyed, and frustrated, but definitely okay.'

'That's what matters.'

He gave her a sideways glance. 'She wanted to meet you. Wanted to hear about your work.'

'Ah, that's nice.' She took a bite of her bagel. 'Maybe some other time. I'd be happy to go over the principles with her. Take it she's having a tough time with this pregnancy?'

He nodded. 'She's one of our most reliable doctors and she's been diabetic since childhood. But since she became pregnant, she's been plagued by unexpected hypoglycaemic attacks. It's a shame. She sat with me at lunch one day, ate everything, then stood up and literally passed out cold.'

'She wasn't showing any signs?'

'About two minutes before she passed out, she got a strange look in her eye—but she was still taking part in the conversation. She's been so well controlled for years that her blood sugar goes really low before she gets any warning signs.'

'Is there nothing they can do?'

Jonas actually looked furtive for a moment and paused.

'What have you done?'

He pulled a face. 'I phoned a company rep that I knew. There's a new thing that's been trialled. It's a patch that fits to the skin and sends a constant cellulose sugar reading to a phone. The phone can alarm for either high or low levels.'

'Did you get one?'

He glanced at his watch. 'Eve—much to her annoyance—is being monitored for a few hours in the antenatal ward. The rep will be here within the hour.'

Cora gave him an interested look. 'You have a good heart, Jonas Nilsson.'

He held out his hands. 'What? She'd do the same for me if I was in that position, and I know it. We're a team. We've got to help each other.'

She gave him a knowing smile. 'That's right.

We're a team. We should help each other. I totally agree.'

The change in her tone of voice got his attention. He set the bagel down. 'Why do I feel like I've just been played?'

Cora shook her head and pointed at the half-eaten bagels. 'Tell me you got us something other than this?'

He sighed and reached into his pocket, pulling out two chocolate bars. Cora took hers, opened it right away and broke off a square of chocolate, putting it in her mouth without pausing for breath.

'You didn't finish your main,' he teased, pointing at the bagel.

She shrugged. 'I like to mix and match. I'll finish them both.' She narrowed her eyes and said warningly, 'Don't try and police my food. Quickest way to make me your enemy.'

'I thought I'd already done that,' he said casually, teasing her.

She ate another piece of chocolate. 'You definitely try my patience. This chocolate might be the only thing that saves you.'

He stopped for a minute, pushing his food away. 'Do we want to talk about what happened between us?'

'The kiss or the fight?'

'Touché. How about both?'

He had her there. Cora wasn't quite sure what to say. Talk about being put on the spot. 'Are you brave enough to go there?' She kind of preferred this casual flirting. Jonas had already learned more about her than most people she'd consider acquaintances. She wasn't entirely sure she wanted to reveal any more.

But on the other hand, finding out a bit more about her mysterious Viking wasn't entirely unappealing.

She licked her lips. 'Okay, then. I'll start with the kiss. I liked it. It was…interesting.'

He sat forward. 'Interesting?' He said the word as if she'd just insulted him.

She smiled at his reaction. 'Yes, it was.'

He frowned. 'Not enticing? Or amazing? I'd even settle for hot.'

Now, she was definitely laughing. 'Well, how would you describe it?'

He folded his arms. 'Unsure.' He was watching her with those pale blue eyes.

'And what does that mean?'

He gave her a half-smile. 'It means I think I need to try again, to be sure.'

'You do?' She couldn't help but smile as he leaned closer.

'I do.' His lips were inches from hers. As she inhaled, she could smell his aftershave.

The soap powder on his uniform. The balm on his skin.

She put her hand on his chest. 'But we haven't got to the fight yet,' she said quietly.

'I thought we could just miss that bit,' he whispered.

'We could,' she agreed, highly tempted. But gave his chest a little push back. 'Or, we could get to the crux of the matter.'

He gave a resigned sigh and sat back on his chair, cracking open his own bar of chocolate. 'Which is?'

'Why you don't like my research or my work.'

He shook his head. 'Your research I don't mind. I've read it all. It's your methods I find... questionable.'

'Questionable?' Her voice rose an octave as he gave her a lazy smile, knowing he'd tempted another reaction out of her.

He waved a hand. 'I think we've established you're a great hands-on doctor. Fearless. Practical. Able to teach. Able to assist in an emergency.'

She gave an approving nod. 'Carry on. I like these thoughts.'

'I thought you might.'

She sighed and waited for him to continue. 'But you don't always see the bigger picture.'

He put his hand on his chest. 'And you don't need to, because that's my job as the manager of this unit and all the staff to make sure that I cross every t and dot every i.'

'Is that a Swedish expression?'

He shook his head. 'No, I looked it up online last night to be able to explain what I meant to you.'

'You planned this conversation last night?' she said with disbelief.

'I planned we'd have it at some point.'

She broke off another piece of chocolate. 'What made you think I'd talk to you again?'

He reached his hand over and touched her skin. 'This.'

There was silence as the little buzz shot up her arm and tickled every sense in her body.

Her eyes were fixed on the spot he'd just touched. 'So, I haven't imagined it,' she said in a low voice.

'No,' he said huskily. 'You haven't imagined it.'

'So what does that mean…for us?'

'It means we have a little less than three weeks left to get to know each other a bit better.' He'd moved closer again, his voice low, his warm breath teasing the skin at her neck.

He smiled at her. 'So, what's it to be? The boat trip, or a visit to the Vasa Museum?'

Something warm stirred inside her heart. He'd remembered. He'd remembered that she didn't love Christmas so much, and wanted to try something different.

That mattered. A lot.

Her green eyes met his gaze. 'You decide,' she said quickly, before sliding her arms around his neck, and sealing the deal with a kiss.

CHAPTER NINE

IT SEEMED THAT he was losing his mind. And Jonas was sure that the gorgeous woman, currently on his arm, was the cause.

This should be harmless. This should be fun. Cora was only here for another few weeks. He already knew that she was due to fly back to London on Christmas Eve.

It had struck him as kind of a sad time of year to travel. But from the casual chats he'd had with Cora, he could tell she wasn't really thinking about it. Others might be fretting about late flights, and delays, and hurrying home to their family, but he already knew Cora didn't like Christmas much, even though he didn't know the finer details.

Today, they were huddled at the entrance to the Vasa Museum—in amongst a long line of tourists. Cora looked up at him with a smile. 'You bring me to all the best places,' she said, her breath turning to steam in the freezing air as she shivered.

He put his arm around her. 'It's warmer once we get inside. Think of this as your cultural experience.'

She laughed. 'It's a chocolate museum, isn't it?'

'You wish. But I know a nice chocolate shop we can visit later.'

'Promises, promises,' she muttered as the line slowly moved forward.

They made their way inside, and it took Cora a few moments to unzip her jacket and realise what was the main exhibit.

She let out a gasp. 'A ship? The Vasa Museum is a ship?'

He smiled and nodded. 'A bit of history. Pay attention. It's the world's only conserved seventeenth-century ship.'

The ship was mounted just above them, so everyone viewing could walk around and underneath and get a feel for the size and quality of the ancient ship.

Cora shook her head. 'How on earth did it get here?'

'It sank,' he said simply. 'A few minutes after being launched in 1628.'

She looked at him in confusion. 'But I still don't get it—this was at the bottom of the sea?'

He nodded. 'After over three hundred years on the sea bed, the *Vasa* was retrieved and preserved for the museum.'

'No way!' she said as she continued to walk underneath. 'No way was this under the sea for three hundred years.' She turned and wagged her finger at him. 'I've watched all those *Titanic* documentaries. Everything just disintegrates. This must be a replica. Isn't it?'

'I'll have you know we Swedes are a talented bunch. Ninety-eight per cent of this ship is original.'

She reached out to try and touch it, even though it was way above her head. 'But...that's impossible.'

He smiled again. He wasn't sure what she'd think of the museum and deliberately hadn't told her what it housed. But it was clear she was impressed. 'Did Vikings sail on it?'

Now, he laughed. 'We'd have to go back a whole lot longer for that. No, it was a warship, and the upper hull was much too heavy. That's why she sank. It's in such good condition because Stockholm has uniquely brackish waters, which basically fossilised the ship and kept her in great condition until her recovery.'

'I can't believe it survived,' said Cora in wonder. She slipped her hand into Jonas's as they continued around the structure.

'Well, a bit like the Titanic, the metal parts suffered. All the iron bolts disintegrated; only things like cannon balls and the anchor survived.' He gave a laugh. 'And the guns and cannons. They were looted years ago.'

Cora slid her jacket off. 'It's quite warm in here.'

'It's kept at a steady temperature to stop the ship deteriorating. If you came in here in the summer, you'd find it chilly and want a jumper.'

'Well, it's so cold outside it feels positively pleasant in here today,' said Cora. They'd walked around the boat twice now.

'Want to visit the restaurant upstairs? The food is quite good here.'

She nodded and passed by an exhibit of the timeline of the ship's preservation as they moved to the stairs. The restaurant was busy already, even though it wasn't quite midday, and they were seated at a table quickly.

'Okay, there's a rule,' said Jonas as the waiter took their drinks order.

'What's the rule?' asked Cora cautiously.

'They have a daily dish here—and it's always Swedish meatballs in a cream sauce with lingonberries. You have to try it.'

Cora smiled. 'I haven't tried any meatballs since I got here.' She picked up the fork at her place setting. 'But I have, of course, tried the meatballs at a very famous store in the UK.'

Jonas groaned and shook his head. 'No, they are an imitation. Now you're in Sweden, you'll try the real thing.'

Jonas ordered for them both as Cora sipped her white wine, and he his beer.

Her mood was good today. He hadn't seen those hidden shadows that occasionally flitted across her eyes. And it was clear she was enjoying herself. She asked questions at an alarming rate, and eventually he had to admit he didn't know all the answers, and bought her a guidebook for the museum.

They joked back and forward as their meal was brought to them and Jonas watched in pleasure as her eyes lit up at the first taste of the genuine Swedish meatballs. She gave a nervous smile. 'I hated to admit that I loved the ones back home, but these are really spectacular.' She leaned back in her chair with a contented glow. 'I swear, if I could come here every day to eat these, I might just move to Stockholm.'

Her words made him curious. 'You've always stayed in London—you wouldn't consider moving elsewhere?'

She shook her head. 'Well, obviously I'm from Scotland, and I trained at Edinburgh

University and worked in the hospitals around there during my training. But, as soon as I qualified, because it's a more specialist field, there just seemed to be more opportunities in London. I had an offer last year of a job in Washington, and then the year before in Germany, but...' she paused as if she were contemplating whether to be honest or not '... I wanted to be in the same part of the world as my sister, Isla, when she was at university. And it's only just over an hour's flight from London. She has her aunt and uncle, of course, but we're close—guess that happens when you're there at the delivery—and I just wanted to be nearby in case she needed me.' She smiled sadly. 'But the truth is, she's all grown up now. She's the most independent girl on the planet. I wouldn't be surprised if she announced she was going to Australia to do her final year of university or something similar.'

Jonas shook his head. 'Wait a minute. Rewind. You were there when Isla was delivered?'

Heat flooded into her cheeks. But she'd said it out loud now. There was no point in lying about it. 'I delivered her. My mum went into labour early, fast, and very unexpectedly. We stayed quite far out in the country. My dad was miles away trading sheep, and it was just me and her.'

Jonas sat back a bit further in his seat. He wanted to know all about this. 'That must have been terrifying. How old were you?'

'Fifteen. Let's just say it was a baptism of fire. The emergency operator was great, calm as you like, and gave me really clear instructions. Isla was born within a few minutes. She was early and needed a bit of assistance with her breathing. The scariest thing was when my mum had a postpartum haemorrhage. I'll never forget seeing all that blood on the floor.'

'What did you do?'

'Exactly what the operator told me to do. They decided to send an air ambulance at that point.'

'How long did that take?'

She gave a distinctly uncomfortable smile. 'Nearly too long. Obviously, I had no oxytocin, and I spent a long time massaging my mum's uterus, trying to get it to contract and stop the bleeding. It was all I could do.'

'Wow, that's brave.'

She nodded slowly. 'In the end, both Isla and my mum were okay. Both stayed in hospital for a few weeks, and it lit a fire in my belly.'

He gave her a strange glance.

'Maybe it's another UK saying. It made me

curious. Made me want to be a doctor. To help small babies like Isla and see if I could learn to do things to help them.' She licked her lips and took a sip of her wine. 'Honestly, it made me who I am today.'

He sat back and watched her for a while, loving the way the sunlight from the windows was catching the tones in her hair, and the glint of her green eyes. She was beautiful. Inside and out. Passionate about her work too. Yes, they might disagree about things, but Cora challenged him. She was the first woman who'd brought some light into his life in the last few years. She made him laugh. She made him furious. And he'd honestly never been so happy around someone.

But somehow he knew there was more—so much more to unravel about this intriguing woman. She still hadn't really told him why she didn't like Christmas, and if he asked now, it would feel like prying. She'd already told him a little of herself, but he was sure there were many more fascinating pieces to the puzzle that made up Cora Campbell. His stomach clenched a little. He'd been burned once before with Katrina. Was he going to let himself be burned again? Could all this blow up in his face?

He took a breath and made an instant decision. He would be patient. He knew Cora still had some secrets. But Jonas hadn't told her everything about himself either. He was rapidly losing his heart to this woman, and, at some point in his life, he had to take the chance. He had to take the chance to be happy.

'What?' she asked.

The word jolted him out of his reverie and he straightened in his chair. 'What?' he countered.

'You were looking at me funny.'

'I was not.'

Her expression was affectionate and her voice lowered. 'Yeah, you were.' Her hands circled the stem of her wine glass. 'So, I've told you what made me who I am. Now you need to reveal a bit of yourself to me.'

It was like being under an instant magnifying glass. He tried the casual wave of his hand. 'Nothing. What you see is what you get.'

She shook her head. 'No, it isn't. Why are you so pedantic at work? Why are you such a stickler for rules and regulations? I get that they're important. I know we have them for safety reasons. But, in my experience, on the odd occasion, it's okay to think outside the box.'

He visibly shuddered and she noticed straight away. 'See? You don't even like those words.'

She paused for a few moments, clearly thinking. Her gaze drifted to the stem of the glass as she stroked her fingers up and down it. 'I've met a few people who act the same way that you do, and all of them had some kind of bad experience at some point in their career that made them a stickler for the rules.'

Her gaze lifted and met his. It was as if she'd just reached her hand into his brain and read everything he kept hidden there. He wanted to deny it. But, for the first time in a long time, someone was reading him like a book.

And it was Cora.

He took a long, slow breath, followed by a sip of his beer. 'Guilty as charged,' he finally said. If he was willing to take a chance with Cora, surely she would be willing to take a chance on him? He knew he was about to reveal the part of himself he didn't talk about much. There was always a deep-down fear that if he revealed this part of himself, a colleague might find him wanting. Might think he'd made the wrong decision and let his patient down. Would Cora?

She gave the slightest shake of her head. 'No. I need more than that.'

He sighed. 'It's just like you said. I had a bad experience. I learned from it. And I do my best to ensure that none of my colleagues end up in the position that I did.'

'And what position was that?'

He looked away from Cora. Her gaze was unnerving.

'I was newly trained as a midwife. Believe it or not, I used to be quite laid-back. I loved being a midwife. I loved working on birth plans and formed really good relationships with my expectant mums.'

'So, what happened?'

He was conscious that she kept gently pushing him to reveal more.

'I had a woman in the late stage of labour. She'd been really clear in her birth plan that she didn't want a Caesarean section unless there was no other choice. She'd had surgery as a child that had left her traumatised and was terrified of undergoing anything similar again. Her birth plan was meticulous. She had control issues, and having every part of her plan detailed in advance helped her feel more in control and helped alleviate her anxiety.'

Cora shook her head. 'Oh, no. I can guess what happened.'

He nodded. 'I made a mistake. I made a promise I eventually couldn't keep. I told her I'd do everything I could to make sure she didn't have a C-section.'

Cora winced. 'Ouch.'

Even now, he could feel a weight pressing down on his shoulders as he talked about the case. 'So, things went just like you'd expect. Baby's heart rate dipped dramatically, the baby was deteriorating and...'

'There was nothing else for it,' Cora finished for him. 'Your patient had to have an emergency C-section.'

He gave an enormous sigh. 'Exactly. And both mum and baby survived.'

'Both healthy?'

He nodded. 'Physically, yes. But mentally? Not so much. For mum, anyway. She complained about me—claimed I'd let her down. She suffered a really severe postnatal depression after the birth of a baby she'd very much wanted.'

'But that could have happened anyway,' said Cora.

'I know that. But I'm sure the whole delivery did affect her mental health.'

'So what happened about the complaint?'

He leaned back in his chair, his hands twisting the napkin on the table. 'I was exonerated. They said that my actions had saved the life of both mum and baby.'

'So why do you look so miserable about it?'

He leaned forward. 'Because I *did* let her

down. I made her a promise that, in the end, I couldn't keep.'

Cora shook her head. 'So, you never had the "what if" conversation with her?'

He frowned. 'Of course, I did. That's how we had it documented that a C-section was only if there was no other choice.'

'And there was no other choice, was there?'

He ran his fingers through his hair. He hated talking about this. 'Of course, there wasn't. But the only thing that saved me in all this was the fact I had documented *everything*. And I'd followed every protocol to the letter. If I'd strayed in any way, they would have found against me.'

Cora held up her hands. 'You did what every good nurse, midwife or doctor does.'

He was still frowning at her. She was saying it as if it made perfect sense.

'Your practice was good, Jonas. You didn't do anything wrong. But that doesn't make you feel any less responsible. Or any less guilty. That's natural. I still remember every patient where there have been questions about care, or a complaint. It doesn't matter that they are few and far between, they stay here—' she pointed to her chest '—inside, grinding and grinding away. Making me ask the "what if" questions constantly. Making me go over every drug prescribed, every conversation I had. Wondering if I didn't read a situation correctly. That's normal. And neither of us would be good practitioners if we didn't reflect. If we didn't try and learn from situations that we wished had turned out differently.'

He gave a slight nod. 'But staff are sometimes slack. They don't understand how important it is to follow all protocols completely. Documentation and safe protocols can, at times, be the difference between a member of staff being charged with something, or not.'

'I know. I get it, I do.' She looked him in the eye. 'But don't you ever just want to park the bad experience, know that you've learned from it, and shake off the guilt? I can still see it sitting there, like a baby elephant in a cloud above your head.'

He let out a surprised laugh at that comment, then instantly became serious again. 'I'm the manager. It's my job to protect my staff.'

Cora agreed. 'It is. But it's also all staff members' professional responsibility to protect themselves. You can't be looking over every shoulder all the time. You can't work twenty-four hours a day.' She held up a cautious finger. 'And remember that we also learn from our mistakes—or our maybe mistakes. Reflecting on those can be even more important. And if you terrify staff with rules, they might be too scared to tell you about mistakes, or about near misses.'

Jonas leaned back, both hands flat on the table, thinking about what she'd just said.

'I can remember as a junior doctor drawing up morphine, double-checking the prescription and the dose with a nurse, then almost giving it to the wrong patient. Someone had swapped beds around while we'd been drawing up the medicine in the treatment room. When we went in to administer the dose, with the chart in our hands, the nurse went to read the name and date of birth from the patient's wristband. I have to admit to not really listening. And it took a few more seconds than normal to realise that something wasn't right.'

'But you didn't give it?'

'No, it didn't even get out of the tray. But for me, that was a near miss.'

He nodded silently and she held up her hand.

'Let me tell you about another. I was part of the arrest team. I got paged to a ward I was unfamiliar with. I reached the scene, and a senior nurse was standing next to a bed, looking stunned. I *assumed* that the nurse had already done the basic ABC checks before she pulled the arrest buzzer. You know…airway, breathing, circulation. So, as the most junior member of the team, I put my knee on the bed and leaned over to start compressions.'

'What happened?'

'I did one, and the elderly patient sat up and said, "Ouch!"'

Jonas put his hand over his mouth. 'She never.'

'Oh, she did. I got the fright of my life and I learned a valuable lesson. Never assume anything.'

'Who pulls an arrest buzzer without doing ABC?'

Cora raised her eyebrows. 'Who, indeed?'

Jonas was still contemplating what she'd said. Could his behaviour mean that staff were reluctant to report things to him? There was an electronic monitoring system in the hospital for any incidents or near misses. It was part of the induction training for any new staff. He'd always just assumed that staff would report the way they should. The thought that his dictate about rules and protocols might actually stop reporting issues was genuinely disturbing.

'Have you seen any incidents that should have been reported and weren't?'

She sighed sadly. 'And that is where the problem lies. Why did your mind go there first? Why didn't your mind say, *Hmm, maybe I should think about that*?'

'It went there too.'

'But that's not what you said.'

He sighed. Boy, she was tough. He put his elbows on the table and leaned forward. 'Okay, I don't want staff to be scared to tell me if something goes wrong.'

Cora nodded and smiled. 'Okay, now we're getting somewhere. I just think you have to strike a balance.'

'How do you feel about a balance?'

'What do you mean?'

'Most of the reasons we've fought is because I think you rush on into things. How about you stop and take a breath too. Try and strike a balance.'

She pulled a face at him for turning her words around on herself. She lifted her glass towards him. 'Maybe we should drink to that?'

The words were out of his mouth in a flash. 'I'd prefer to seal the deal with a kiss.'

She blinked and licked her lips. Once. And then twice.

And then she stood up and walked around the table towards him. He stood to greet her.

'Deal.' She smiled, as she stood on tiptoe to plant a kiss on his lips.

For a moment he thought it was going to be a fleeting kiss. But his body reacted immediately, bringing his hands to her waist and pulling her close. Cora's hands wound around his neck and their kiss deepened. They were in a public space so he couldn't do exactly what he wanted to do. But as he kissed her he breathed in her shampoo, her body lotion and her light perfume, a collision of floral scents that invaded his very pores.

She pulled her lips back, smiling, and murmured in a low voice, 'Sometimes, it's worth the wait.' Her warm breath caressed his skin. She rested her forehead against his cheek.

He laughed quietly. 'More than worth it,' he said as he stepped back with the sexiest smile on his face that she'd ever seen.

CHAPTER TEN

CORA STRETCHED OUT in her hotel bed and smiled. Last night they'd gone to see a movie in English and she'd eaten popcorn and drunk soda with her head on Jonas's shoulder.

The day before, flowers had been delivered to her hotel room. The beautiful pink and white blooms had started to open and the aroma was drifting across the air towards her.

Today, they were going to one of the Christmas markets. That would mean coffee and cake, and a chance to see all the items for sale. She jumped out of bed and quickly dressed in a warm green jumper she'd bought the other day that was threaded through with glitter. She pulled on her jeans and boots and wrapped a checked scarf around her neck. She was just sliding her arms into her green coat when there was a knock at her door.

'Ready to go shopping?' she asked Jonas,

whose frame filled her doorway in a way that was far too inviting.

He leaned down and kissed her. 'New jumper?'

She nodded and pulled it out. 'Isn't it fabulous? I saw it in a shop window on the way home the other night and had to dash in and buy it. It's the perfect colour—even matches the coat you bought me.'

As she zipped her coat and grabbed her gloves, she ran a hand down the front of the jacket. 'You know, I've worn this every day since you bought me it.' She gave him a wink. 'It's brought me good luck.'

'Luck has nothing to do with it,' said Jonas as he pulled her forward for another kiss. 'I just have incredibly good taste.'

She kissed him in agreement and grabbed her bag. 'Should we go for breakfast first?'

'Oh, no!' He laughed. 'Wait until we get to the market. There will be food galore.'

It was only a short walk to the square where the Christmas market was held. There were a few across the city, but Jonas had suggested this was the best place to start.

There were around forty stalls, all red-painted wood, with a whole variety of items, and, true to his promise, the first thing Cora noticed was the delicious smell of food.

The place was already busy, both with tourists and locals. 'Where do we start?'

Jonas reached over and took her hand, threading their way through the crowd and stalls and finally stopping at one where the vendor was making pancakes. 'How about here?'

'Oh, wow.' They ordered coffee and pancakes, which were served on a wobbly paper plate. Cora tucked the coffee into her elbow and ate her pancakes as they drifted between all the other stalls.

'No way,' she whispered in horror to Jonas as she pointed at a sign. 'That can't be true.'

He grinned. 'Reindeer sausages? Oh, it's true. They're actually really popular.'

'You eat Rudolph?'

He didn't even blink. 'And Dasher, and Prancer, and Vixen, and whatever the rest of them are called.'

Cora shuddered and moved on. The next stall had Christmas cheese, crispbreads and handmade mustard. 'This is much more like it,' she said as she tried a few samples. The next had sugared almonds, honey, marzipan, *pepparkakor*—ginger snaps—saffron buns, homemade jams and marmalades and penny candy. Cora was highly tempted, but groaned. 'Those pancakes and that taste of cheese have ruined me. Take me away from all this food and show me things that can't do me any harm.'

He laughed and directed her to a range of other stalls all carrying different goods. Christmas music was playing as they wandered around the various stalls. She could even hear a few carols being sung. But Cora was completely distracted by the tall blond on her arm. Everything else seemed to dull around him.

Every now and then, people would come up and speak to him. More than one had a small child in their arms or trailing after them. It was clear from the faces of the mothers and fathers that these were children and parents who Jonas had met through work.

One woman threw her hands around his neck and kissed him on both cheeks, talking rapidly. Jonas took it all in his stride, happily meeting the twins she had in a double buggy and introducing Cora to the two little girls. She was impressed that he remembered the names of both the mother and the girls instantly and was completely at ease. When the woman finally left she turned to him. 'Another patient?'

He nodded. 'Long-standing patients. Twins were born very early. They are still under our monitoring programme.'

'Of course, I did. Your staff are a great bunch. I love working with them.'

'Then why don't you stay?'

It was clear that the words had come from nowhere and seemed to shock Jonas just as much as they shocked Cora.

He seemed to take a breath and then added on a slightly more serious note, 'I suspect that Stockholm City will be advertising for a new clinical Head of Neonatology in the next few months.'

'You don't think Elias will be back?'

He sighed, and she could see the pain on his face. 'Truthfully? I'd love him to come back. But I'm not sure that he'll want to. I'm sure his son and daughter will try and persuade him to retire. He might want to return a few days a week. But I think the running of the unit will all be too much for him.' He locked gazes with her again. 'So, at some point soon, I suspect we'll be looking for a new clinical lead.'

She was watching him carefully: he'd been partly shocked by his first direct invitation, but now she could see the idea start to settle on him.

'I'm not sure I would be the best person for the job,' she said, her automatic defensive mechanisms kicking into place. She wasn't

'The same one that the babies who've had therapeutic hypothermia will go on?'

He nodded. 'We nurse these patients for so long, I'm always interested in the long-term outcomes.' He wrapped an arm around her shoulder. 'No matter what you think of me, I get paged when any of our previous long-term patients come in for review, and I always do my best to go along and say hello, then talk to the paediatrician later.'

She gave him a curious glance. 'Is this official, or unofficial?'

He waggled his free hand in the air in front of them. 'Let's just say it's both personal and professional interest.'

'I knew you were a secret softy at heart,' she said as they moved over to the other range of stalls. They browsed easily. Cora bought some hand-knitted mittens that were the same colour as her jumper and parka, some white and red glassware, and a couple of Christmas-scented candles. She inhaled deeply as she chose them. 'I'll take these home,' she said. 'They'll remind me of being here.'

Something inside her stomach twisted painfully. Although she loved Stockholm, she'd found the time of year tough, as always. But now, the thought of going back to her empty flat in London didn't fill her with joy. Sure, it would be nice to sleep in her own bed again. But the bed at the hotel had been very comfortable. The staff at the hotel were lovely and hospitable, and she got that genuine vibe from the city too. By the time she flew home, it would be almost Christmas Day, and, unless she asked someone back home to help her out, she'd be arriving home to a relatively cold flat with no food. She'd already turned down the invite to go to her aunt and uncle's in the Highlands—mainly because the travel would be too complicated.

Jonas put a hand on her shoulder. 'You okay?' His gentle voice was like a warm hug around her heart.

'Of course.' She smiled. 'More shopping?'

There it was again. That odd expression on his face for the briefest of seconds. Then he gave her another smile and put his hand around her shoulder again. It was starting to become colder. Behind them the school choir started to sing more carols as they wandered past a market stall with traditional reusable Swedish advent calendars.

Cora was half tempted to stop and look. It had been a long time since she'd had an advent calendar, and these ones could be filled with tiny gifts.

'Want one?' Jonas asked.

She shook her head and watched as a woman walked past with a delicious-looking bag of chocolates.

'I'd like one of those, though.'

'Oh, I know exactly where that stall is. Let's go.'

He took her around to the back of the stalls, then across the road to a glass-fronted exclusive chocolatier. As soon as he pushed open the door and her senses were hit by the delicious scents, she couldn't help the wide smile that spread across her face.

'You said it was a market stall.'

'I might have been a stranger to the truth.'

'This place costs a fortune, doesn't it?' she whispered.

'Absolutely.' He nodded.

An aproned assistant appeared and happily guided Cora around the huge range of single chocolates on display. She couldn't help herself, and picked a whole range that were wrapped in a gold box with a flamboyant red bow. As they exited the store she turned to Jonas. 'I think I've just been very, very bad.'

'It's allowed,' he said.

She shook her head. 'No, what I mean is, I'm going to take them into the NICU. The staff might be distracted for the next day or so.'

'You bought them for the staff?'

entirely sure if he was suggesting the job, or maybe something else.

'Think you're not smart enough?' he joked quickly.

She rolled her eyes as they started to walk again. 'I definitely don't have a good enough handle on the language.'

'Try some immersive therapy,' he nudged. 'People always say it's the best way to learn. Move to a place, spend all day there, and try and speak the language constantly.' He gave a wicked grin. 'Or, there are some other immersive therapies we could consider.'

'Cheeky,' she nudged him right back, then stopped walking and looked around. 'It's a beautiful city, but I don't know enough about it yet. I know I've stayed at a great hotel. But I'd need to find out about renting or buying, where the good areas are, where the not so good are. The driving arrangements if I wanted to get a car. The living costs. Everything, really.'

'Sounds like you're trying to talk yourself out of the possibility.'

She gave a rueful shrug. 'I'm just not sure. I'd need to think about Isla. I know it's a short flight, but it's still a whole other country. Anyhow, we don't even know if a job will come up. There could be other amazing candidates.

People that your hospital might go out to with offers, rather than advertise the job.'

He nodded his head slowly. She froze. The way he was looking at her was...unnerving.

'Is that what you're doing?' Every tiny hair on her body was standing on end.

The expression on his face told her everything she needed to know. 'They mentioned it to me yesterday. Gave me a few names that the board might consider. Asked what I thought of them.'

Something clicked in Cora's brain. She raised her eyebrows. 'But I wasn't one of them, was I?'

The pause was excruciating. 'No,' he admitted. 'But I think you should be.'

She leaned forward and grabbed the lapels of his jacket, heaving him towards her in the busy street. 'Jonas Nilsson, you didn't even consider me until right now, did you?'

He sighed as his arms folded around her. 'The truth is, I didn't consider *anyone* apart from doctors who are the heads of surrounding NICUs in Sweden.'

Cora held her arms above her head. 'But there's a whole world out there.'

He bowed his head and closed his eyes. 'I know that. But I think when any job comes up, you immediately look at all those you've worked with, and those close by. Heads of units that we speak to frequently because of transfers, or crib shortages, or imminent arrivals.'

She tilted her head to one side as she smiled up at him. Cora was feeling a little easier. For a few moments, she'd felt really on the spot. As if Jonas were asking about a whole lot more than a job. 'Think of all the wonderful people you might miss, thinking like that,' she teased.

He dipped his head, his slight bristles brushing the side of her cheek. 'And think of all the opportunities you might miss if you only look at the UK for job opportunities.'

'Touché.' She smiled and now he laughed out loud, knowing that she was teasing him about his word choice a few weeks ago.

She stared up into those pale blue eyes and her heart gave a little leap. What about staying here, living here, and working here? Jonas was the first guy she'd met in for ever who made her catch her breath, who made her skin tingle with one glance, and who challenged her, day and night. The sparks flew when they were in a room together. She liked it that he didn't always agree with her, and wasn't afraid to say so. Of course, he was wrong, but that didn't matter.

A tiny sprig unfurled deep inside her. The one that had been there since childhood. The one that told her she wasn't good enough, wasn't loved enough, to take up a post like this. She hated that it always appeared at times like this. Jonas hadn't thought of her first. He'd been working with her side by side—if he really thought she was good enough he should have thought of her first.

She pushed the feelings aside. He'd thought of her *now*. That was what was important. And he was enthused about it. Even though she didn't know if she wanted the job. The sprig inside was turning into something else— a beautiful rose.

'What are you thinking about?'

She smiled. 'A world of opportunities,' she admitted. She took a breath. 'I'm kind of cold. Want to come back to the hotel with me?'

He bent down again and whispered in her ear, 'I thought you'd never ask,' and slipped his hand into hers.

They walked along the street together, and she was conscious that her footsteps seemed to be quickening. She kept a firm hold of his hand when they reached the hotel entrance and she nodded to the doorman and receptionist as they crossed the lobby to the lift.

As soon as the doors slid closed, Jonas was kissing her again.

Now they weren't in public. He pressed her

up against the mirrored wall of the lift and she wrapped her arms tightly around him as he kissed her until she was breathless.

When the lift slowed to a halt and pinged she stepped back and looked at him again. Her mouth was dry. But she knew exactly what she wanted the next step to be.

She licked her lips and held out her hand. 'Stay over.'

He hesitated, and for a second she felt a wave of panic. Was she overreaching? Misreading things between them?

But Jonas let out a soft laugh as the doors opened to her floor.

'Like I said earlier, I thought you'd never ask,' he said again, as this time he grabbed her round the waist, lifted her up and she wrapped her legs around him.

Cora couldn't help but laugh as she struggled to find her card for the door. 'Maybe a little unconventional?' she teased.

Jonas took it from her hand as she found it and swiped the door, carrying her inside and kicking it shut behind them.

Her heart swelled. A perfect day, and things could only get better.

CHAPTER ELEVEN

THEY'D QUICKLY FALLEN into routine. One night they would spend a night at Cora's hotel, then the next they would wake up together in Jonas's apartment.

He was surprised how quickly she seemed to fit into his life—in lots of weird ways. It felt entirely normal to see her snuggled up at the end of his pale grey sofa, or under the white blankets in his large bed. Within a few days her toothbrush remained in his bathroom, and he'd bought an extra one to leave in her hotel room.

'So, how're things going in love's young dream?'

The words jerked him from his thoughts. Alice was standing next to him in the NICU with a set of older notes in her hands. She was giving him 'that' look. The one that told him she could read every thought in his head and knew exactly everything he'd been up to in the last few weeks.

'I have no idea what you're talking about, Alice,' he said, doing his best to keep his face straight.

'Of course, you don't.' She smiled, patting his hand as she moved over to the computer screen.

'That's why you watch every step she takes, turn your head every time she laughs, and notice every time she talks to another member of staff.' She raised her eyebrows just an inch. 'And she, it seems, does entirely that same with you. The vibe between you both has changed.' She stepped a little closer and lowered her voice. 'And in case you think it's a secret...' she shook her head '...just so you know, we've been taking bets for a while.'

Jonas tried not to look stunned, but clearly failed when Alice started to quietly laugh. After another minute, he folded his arms. 'Who won?'

There was no chance for an answer as one of the alarms started to ping dangerously. As if by magic, all the staff in the unit moved smoothly. Resuscitating a tiny baby was always a delicate operation. One staff member automatically went to mum and put her arm around her, while moving her back, away from the crib, so others could do what they needed to.

Jonas and Alice joined the team, doing tiny heart compressions, bagging the tiny little boy and administering emergency medications, until finally the heart monitor started to blip reassuringly. A few moments later, the little boy's chest started to rise and fall rapidly as breathing was re-established, and his blood pressure started to come back up.

It was another hour before Jonas and Alice were back near the nurses' station. The phone rang and he answered it. 'Jonas, we've another baby on the way up. Meets all the criteria. Can you be ready? I'll be up in five.'

He put the phone down and gave Alice a nod. 'Another baby for the hypothermia treatment. Cora is on her way up.'

'Oh, is she?' said Alice wickedly, all the while moving off to prepare one of the side rooms.

Jonas shook his head as he moved after her. 'Is this what it's come to? Is this what I'm going to have to put up with at work every day?'

Alice grabbed a drip stand to pull into the room and threw him an interested look as she attached the machine to the stand. 'You have no idea how much pleasure it gives me.

How much pleasure it gives us all.' Her hand reached over to his arm as he was preparing the crib. 'Jonas, you seem so happy around her. Mad at times. Then delighted at others. Honestly, if you let this one get away, I'll make your life a misery afterwards.'

The words stopped him cold. He looked at the older woman, who might have made a million mistakes in her life, but he'd never know it. Her gaze was honest, sincere and playful all at once. It yanked at every heartstring he'd ever had.

'You wouldn't have to, Alice. I'd be there already.' The honesty of the words was like a bucket of ice-cold water emptying over his head.

He was frozen. Thinking about how much Cora actually meant to him.

Alice was routinely going about her business. 'Have you told her?'

His eyes darted to Alice. She was so cool and casual about things—as if this were an everyday conversation that they were having.

But it wasn't. And they both knew it.

He loved the way she could be so matter-of-fact about things. It was one of her greatest traits, and why the entire hospital staff looked up to the experienced sister of the NICU. She was unflappable, to the point, entirely professional, and all with a little gleam in her eye.

The slightly scary thing was, he knew she would make his life a misery if he didn't up his game and speak to Cora.

So he was entirely honest with her. 'Of course, I haven't told her. She's due to go back—' He stopped as something came into his head. He'd been about to say 'back home', but realised that he got the general impression from Cora that, right now, nowhere really felt like home to her. 'She's due to go back to London in two weeks.'

'Sounds like you're running out of time, Jonas.'

He shook his head as he plugged in some of the other pieces of equipment. 'Yeah, don't rub it in, Alice.'

She bumped him with her hip on the way past. 'Don't say I didn't warn you.'

The NICU doors flew open and Jonas pushed everything out of his head. It didn't help that Cora's face was the first one he saw, and he instantly drank in everything about her. It was amazing how quickly she'd got under his skin, and he didn't mind one bit.

But as he worked methodically, helping the team get set up for the treatment, his mind kept going back to Cora. He'd already unexpectedly asked her if she'd considered staying, and it was abundantly clear it had never crossed her mind.

To be honest, until that point, it hadn't crossed his either. But as soon as it had landed there, it had just made perfect sense, and it had made his heart lurch in a way that had surprised him.

But inside his head, there were a few tiny doubts. His judgement had been wrong before. His ex had proved that. And every time he saw Cora loaded down with shopping bags, it just rang alarm bells in his head. She'd done and said absolutely nothing to make him think she could be anything like Kristina. But then again, Kristina had done nothing to raise alarm bells either. Maybe his whole judgement was just questionable?

And if he couldn't get past that, how could he have any other kind of conversation with Cora? He shook his head as he put some recordings on a chart. He'd told Cora the most significant event in his life. And she'd talked it through with him with empathy, understanding and reassurance. She hadn't doubted his practice for a single second. And that meant something to him. But could he actually say those three little words to her? Last time around it had spelled disaster for him. Could he be brave enough to try again?

As the team set to work, lowering the new baby's temperature, he moved out of the room to let them continue their work. The start-up procedures were the most labour intensive and, once they were over, the unit settled down to a steady hum of activity. There, in the waste basket near him, were the remnants of a box of chocolates with a familiar logo. The first box Cora had brought in had disappeared in one day. She'd bought a second, and this was clearly the remnants of the third. It struck a chord with him about how she felt about the staff here. They'd wanted to learn from her, and it was clear she relished the opportunity. How would he really feel if Cora was a permanent fixture around here?

Jonas grabbed his jacket and took a walk. He was already long over the hours he should have worked and wanted to clear his head.

Snow crunched under his feet as he walked towards the city centre. Lights glowed everywhere. Before he knew it, he was outside her hotel—the one he'd taken her to on that first day. Cora was still back in the unit. He knew that. He took a few moments to walk around the square. Another Christmas tree had appeared, decorated with pink lights. There seemed to be trees all over the city this year. He hadn't got around to putting his own up back at his apartment. He was usually a bit more festive. But he knew there were still more layers to Cora Campbell. She'd told him she didn't like Christmas much, and it had seemed wrong to push it on her by decorating his apartment. She'd remarked that she frequently just closed the curtains in her room at the hotel to block it out.

As Jonas watched other tourists and some local families walk past, his heart was sad. Christmas wasn't for everyone and he could accept that. But what he really wanted to do was to make some new memories for Cora. Give her something else to think about. He'd already suggested it, but he still wasn't sure if she wanted to take him up on that.

As much as he wanted to do something, he knew deep inside he had to let that be Cora's decision to make. He had no idea what her experience of Christmas had been, or if she was ready to try something new.

Something flooded over him like a wash of warm water in the icy cold. Even though he'd compared Cora and Kristina in his head, he knew in his heart that Cora was nothing like Kristina. They weren't even in the same ballpark. And even though he'd said those three words to Kristina in the past, the way he felt about Cora couldn't even compare. It was so much more. So much better. So much fuller. Any feelings he'd had for Kristina were a pale comparison to what he felt about Cora.

This was love, pure, unadulterated love.

As he walked past a nearby shop, something in the window caught his eye. Before he had time to think much longer, he ducked inside, coming out five minutes later with the gift tucked in his pocket. Would she like it?

He wasn't sure. He could only wait to find out. Because he knew what he needed to say to her. He just had to find a way to let those words out again. His heart knew exactly how he felt about Cora. But could he actually tell her?

Cora looked around the unit. The little boy, Sam, was steady now. She'd been seriously concerned about him earlier, and she could only hope that the treatment would help him. Now, she needed to find Jonas. Something had happened today, and she wanted to tell him, and get a sense of what he thought.

'Anyone know where Jonas has gone?' she asked one of the nearby staff nurses.

The girl turned to a colleague and held up her hand for a high five. He slapped it and they both laughed. 'What?' asked Cora.

The nurse shook her head. 'We've just been

waiting for confirmation—but it doesn't really matter, we already knew.'

Cora smiled. 'So, does anyone know where Jonas has gone?'

She nodded. 'He headed out earlier. I think he said something about a walk. He'd been here for around twelve hours; he probably needed some head space.'

Cora wrinkled her nose. When she'd woken this morning, Jonas had been gone with a scribbled cute note next to her bed. She'd just imagined he'd had some things to do. She hadn't realised he'd come into work early.

She made a few final checks, then grabbed her jacket, zipping it up and pulling out her phone to text Jonas. He answered straight away, and as she pushed open the doors of the unit, something came into her head. She looked over her shoulder. 'Okay, then, who just won the bet?'

'Alice,' they both answered in unison.

'Of course.' She nodded. 'I should have known.'

She couldn't stop smiling as she left the hospital and headed to meet Jonas. It was dark, but the streets seemed even busier than normal.

Jonas appeared through the crowd and slung an arm around her shoulder. 'Do you remember that boat tour I promised you?'

She nodded. 'But it's dark, I won't see anything.'

'This is a special tour. Perfect for night time. We cross under twelve different bridges and see most of the city.' He bent down and whispered in her ear. 'There's even Swedish *fika* on board.'

'Coffee and cinnamon buns? You got me.'

They boarded the boat at Strömkajen. Cora stood at the railing on the boat and watched as the white craft pulled out into the black water. All around them, across the city, white lights were sparkling, outlining buildings, and giving the whole city a glow. Soft music played in the background as a guide gave them a little information about the history of the city, and the bridges they passed underneath. They even passed through the lock that connected the Baltic Sea to Lake Mälaren.

As it got colder, they ducked inside and grabbed some coffee and a cinnamon bun. 'Want to sit down?' Jonas asked.

She shook her head. 'Actually, I'm really enjoying this. Can we take these outside?'

He nodded and they went back to the railing. Cora watched the wonder of the passing sights. The inner city, the Old Town, Södermalm and Lilla glided past. Her heart was warm. The twinkling festive lights only added to the experience. She put her head on Jonas's shoulder. Between the steam from their breaths, and the steam from their coffee cups, it made the cold night air seem even more special.

She was starting to love this city, and the people in it. For the first time in for ever, the thought of Christmas didn't fill her with sadness and dread. Jonas had suggested—without asking tricky questions—that it might be time to make some new memories. And somehow, being in an entirely new place, with a wonderful man and a great bunch of staff, was making it a whole lot easier. Maybe it was timing too. But it was almost as if the dark cloud that seemed to descend around her shoulders at this time of year had forgotten where she was.

Snuggling up with Jonas, and looking out at this new place, was perfect.

'Hey.' His lips brushed her ear. 'What's up?'

She turned towards him and slid her hands around his waist. 'Nothing's up,' she said with a smile on her face. 'I'm just happy.'

'Happy?' He pulled her closer. 'Now, that sounds good.'

She nodded. 'One of the directors of the hospital came and found me today.'

He didn't look particularly surprised. 'They did?'

She gave his chest a gentle slap. 'They told

me that—as well as another suite of candidates—they were considering me for the position of Head of Neonatology.' Her voice was shaking a little.

'And what did you say?'

She stood on her tiptoes and kissed one of his cheeks. 'I listened carefully...' she kissed the other cheek '...and said thank you very much...' she dropped a soft kiss on his lips '...and that I'd wait to hear from them.'

She slid her arms around his neck. 'Do you think someone put in a good word for me?'

He gave her a small smile. 'They might have.'

'But is there any chance that person might be a bit biased?'

He laughed. 'It doesn't matter if I'm biased. The board listens to lots of people. They'll have spoken to your colleagues back at the Royal Kensington, they'll have asked many of the other professionals you've worked with over the last few weeks. They want someone they know will fit well with the unit. Someone who can help us maintain our standards and reputation.'

She let her fingers run through his hair. 'You think someone like me—a woman who makes your blood boil at times—can do that?'

He slid one hand under her thick jacket.

'Sometimes blood boiling means a totally different thing,' he said with a soft laugh.

She pressed closer as she looked over his shoulder. 'This place has been surprising. I've never really considered a proper move before. Even when I was offered a job in Washington a few years ago, I never truly, really considered it properly.'

'And now you will?'

She nodded and pressed her lips together. 'If they ask me.'

'Will you talk to your sister first?'

She blinked back some tears and nodded. 'Absolutely. But I have a feeling that Isla will tell me to chase my dreams.'

'And what are your dreams?'

The question circled around her brain. She immediately wanted to say that she didn't know. But, deep down, parts of her did know. Jonas drove her crazy and she loved that. She'd never wanted to be around someone so much. Waking up next to him every morning had quickly given her the vibe that she was entirely in the right place.

But could she trust him with her heart?

She wanted to. She really, really did.

CHAPTER TWELVE

'HEY, HOW ARE you doing?' Jonas leaned forward and put his hands on Elias's shoulders, kissing him on either cheek as he opened the door.

Elias looked distinctly shaky. He had a stick in one hand and had limped slowly to the door. 'How's my unit?'

'Interesting,' said Jonas as he followed Elias inside and closed the door behind him. His heart fell as he saw a few boxes piled up in one corner. It told him everything he needed to know. But for Elias's sake, he pretended he hadn't seen them as they walked slowly through to Elias's large kitchen and sat down at the table. Jonas noticed that the coffee was already made.

He sat a bag on the table and started emptying it. 'Favourite marmalade, bread, biscuits, and those peppermint creams that you hide in your top desk drawer.'

Elias smiled, and Jonas breathed another sigh of relief. Both sides of his face were moving in perfect symmetry.

His hand shook a little as he determinedly poured the coffee. Another sign. These hands that had inserted thousands of central lines over the years into tiny veins would not be doing that again.

He kept all emotion from his face. He knew that Elias's heart must be breaking. Work had been such a huge part of his life after his wife had died. And now that had been taken from him too.

'What do you mean by interesting?' asked Elias. 'How's the new doctor working out?' There. He had a glint in his eye. The main part of Elias was completely intact.

Jonas couldn't help the smile spreading across his face. 'She's good. Feisty. Challenging. But definitely an excellent doctor.'

'Asked her out yet?'

Jonas choked on his coffee. 'What?'

'A bright, intelligent, good-looking woman? What's wrong with you? From the first second I spoke to her, I thought you would be an excellent match.'

Jonas was incredulous. 'You invited a doctor to our hospital because you thought she would be a good match for me?'

Elias shook his head. 'Of course not. I invited her purely because of her research—which is outstanding, and I hope you've got everything set up for us to continue when she leaves. The match part came later. That video conferencing is a fine thing. Her manner. The passion for her job. That accent. She isn't married, is she? Because I thought she would be perfect for you. I'm just annoyed I haven't got to play matchmaker and take full credit for it.'

He dipped one of the biscuits that Jonas had brought in his coffee.

'You're an old rogue.'

Elias's eyes shimmered with pride. 'I knew it. You do like her.'

He sat back in his chair and gave a self-satisfied sigh. Then, his expression changed. This time his face was full of sadness. 'I tendered my resignation last week. But you know that, don't you?'

Jonas nodded his head. 'I suspected. The board of directors approached me about possible candidates for Head of Neonatology.'

Elias looked interested. 'Who did you recommend?'

'Franz Kinnerman from Lindesberg, Ruth Keppell from Lund, Astra Peniker from Kalmar…' He paused for a second. 'And Cora Campbell from the Kensington.'

Elias tapped his fingers on the table and nodded. 'I also recommended two out of the three. But I asked them to pay particular attention to the performance of our visiting consultant.'

He smiled at Jonas. 'I take it my matchmaking is going well?'

Jonas took a breath. He wasn't quite sure how to answer.

'Come now, Jonas. Tell me you've put that whole episode with Kristina behind you. It's time to make new horizons for yourself. Take a chance on love again.'

Jonas shook his head. Elias was one of the only people he'd confided in about what had happened with Kristina. He reached over and grabbed a biscuit. 'I don't remember asking for love advice.'

Elias tapped his hand on Jonas's arm. 'But I won't be around much longer to give it to you.' His expression changed again. 'My son has persuaded me to sell up and move down next to him and his wife.' Elias looked around his home with the wide windows showing the land around about him. 'Forty years I've lived here. But all good things…' He met Jonas's gaze again. 'It's for the best. But who will be here to keep an eye on you and give you advice about life? I feel as if I should leave you in a safe, but sparky pair of hands. And I think they are distinctly Scottish.'

Jonas burst out laughing. 'Wait until I tell Cora you called her sparky.'

'You should have brought her with you today. I would have liked to have seen you two together. See if there really are sparks flying.'

Jonas was serious now. 'She asked. She wanted to come and meet you. I told her I had to wait until I'd seen how you are.'

'Well, bring her back when she wants to know more about running the unit. I'll give her all the tips she'll need. Or...' there was a wicked gleam in his eyes '...you could always just invite me to the wedding.'

'Elias!'

'What?' He held up his hands, his face the picture of innocence. 'Can't let a good one slip away. And Christmas is always such a lovely time of year for a proposal. It's when I proposed to Ann, you know. Under the giant Christmas tree at Skeppsbron.'

Jonas took a sip of his coffee. 'Christmas isn't her favourite time of year. I don't exactly know why. I didn't want to push. I just suggested that since she was in a new place, it might be nice to make some new memories.'

'With a new person?' Elias gave a nod. 'Wise man. But you should ask. Always ask the difficult questions, Jonas. Then she'll know you care. That you want the good, and the bad.' He gave a soft smile. 'But you know that, don't you? You only have a few days left—don't leave it too late.'

Jonas nodded slowly. 'Let's just say, I have a plan.'

He glanced at his watch. 'I'll have to run. I'm the duty manager at the hospital this afternoon.' He stood up and reached over and gave Elias a giant hug. 'Next time I come, I promise I'll bring Cora with me.'

'Be sure you do.'

Jonas pulled on his jacket and left, pausing outside for a moment to take a deep breath. So much of what Elias had said to him rang true.

But what was most important was that he was right. Time was running out.

And it was time to look to the future.

CHAPTER THIRTEEN

SOMEONE HAD PRESSED fast forward on her life. Last time she'd looked at the calendar there had still been nearly two weeks left in her time here.

But it felt as if she'd blinked—and that time had gone.

Every night had seemed shorter than the one before. Waking up next to Jonas had become excruciating because she'd realised that soon it wouldn't be happening any more.

She'd spoken to Isla the other day, who'd told her she was spending Christmas with their aunt and uncle and wouldn't be coming down to London.

Cora had made a half-hearted scramble to look at when her flight got into London, and any possible chance of reaching the Highlands safely, even though she'd known it was completely futile. Alternative flights to Inverness airport were full. It seemed that most of the Highlands wanted to get home on Christmas Eve.

But what she couldn't get out of her head was the dark cloud that continually settled around her shoulders at this time of year. It had arrived again—even though she'd hoped it wouldn't.

Being in Stockholm had been the perfect distraction at first. But maybe it was time to accept that, no matter what else was going on in her life, she would never get over these feelings associated with Christmas.

And this, doubled with the fact that she hadn't quite managed to figure out exactly how she felt about Jonas—or how he felt about her—was making her lose sleep at night. She should be over the moon with the time she was spending with him. But now it just felt like a double countdown looming over her head. The countdown to bad memories. And the countdown to leaving Jonas behind.

She hadn't heard anything about the job, which likely meant they had another preferred candidate. It would seem ridiculous to let her go back to London, and then offer the job to her. And even that was completely crazy. She hadn't come to Stockholm even thinking about the possibility of a job change. It hadn't been on her radar at all. But, after falling in love with Stockholm, and the staff at City hospital, and falling in love with Jonas, she had such mixed feelings about going back home.

Cora froze. She was tying her shoelaces and her hands just stuck in mid-air. She *loved* Jonas. She loved him. The thought had entered her brain so easily, and the realisation struck her like a blow to the chest.

She sat back up and let out some slow breaths. It was early evening, Jonas would be here in a while, but she'd planned to go for some fresh air. She grabbed her jacket, and looked out at the square, and blinked back a few tears.

Did she really want to go out there? In amongst the glistening white lights and people excited about Christmas?

She pulled her hat over her head and grabbed her gloves. As soon as she reached the foyer of the hotel, the receptionist shouted her over. All the staff knew her by name now. There was a large tray of cookies on the reception desk and Cora could smell them instantly.

'Help yourself, Cora. They've just come up from the kitchen. They're still warm.'

Cora smiled. 'They smell delicious. Thank you.'

'We'll really miss you when you head back to England. Will you come and visit again?'

It was like a little light going on in her head. She'd been so encompassed by the thoughts of going home, and everything that was ending for her, that she hadn't even thought of her holiday time. Wow. Her head must be really muddled.

'I'd love to come back again, and if I do, I promise I'll stay here.' Her footsteps felt a little lighter as she walked out to the square and started to meander her way around in the dimming evening light.

The shop window displays were all familiar to her now, and she couldn't pretend that she didn't have favourites. The traditional carved pale wooden trees behind a white chequered window were lovely. Another shop had a whole array of small glass ornaments with splashes of colour. The effects were mesmerising. She'd already bought a little sculpture with splashes of green, and a mini square with a pink drop in the middle. Now a wall hanging with a flash of red across the middle was catching her eye. It was the size of a large dinner plate—did she have enough space in her luggage? Who cared? She could buy another suitcase if needed.

She continued along the street, stopping to buy a soft grey jumper for Isla, and a decorative studded bangle.

The air was icy and there were several stalls

set up in the middle of the square. She wandered over and decided to be brave and try another cup of warm *glögg*. She sat down on a bench, ignoring the cold as she watched the world go by.

She wasn't even seeing the Christmas decorations now. She was just seeing the people. The families and couples, all walking along laughing and joking. Tears blinked in her eyes as she saw a man and a woman with a teenager and a baby in a buggy. It gave her instant flashbacks to what her family must have looked like to others.

And before she knew it, she was in floods of tears.

'Cora!' The joyful shout came from the other side of the square. Jonas looked really happy. He practically sprinted across the square to join her, and she quickly wiped her tears away.

'I wanted to talk to you,' he said, slightly breathless, a wide grin across the face that she loved.

'What is it?'

There was a weird kind of pause. He sat down on the bench next to her and looked as if he was trying to decide where to start. He bent down and kissed her. Cora responded instantly, because Jonas's touch to her was as natural as breathing air.

When they separated, his arm was still around her shoulders. 'Have you made a decision?'

Her stomach squeezed. 'About what?'

'About where we're going for dinner tonight?'

Every muscle in her body sagged. For some strange reason she'd hoped it would be an entirely different question. Have you made a decision about wanting to stay here? Have you made a decision about when you're coming back? Have you made a decision about what happens next for us?

But maybe she was just imagining the connection between them both. After all, she'd only just realised herself that she loved this man. They hadn't talked about love. They hadn't talked about anything to do with when her time with the Kensington Project was up. And that suddenly struck her as odd.

If Jonas felt the same way she did, surely he would have started a conversation with her by now?

For reasons she couldn't entirely explain, tears started rolling down her cheeks again. It was as if every emotion had just burst to the surface and was overwhelming her.

Maybe he thought she wasn't good enough for him. Maybe he didn't want her the way she hoped he did. Maybe, yet again, she would be the child left alone at Christmas. The feelings were overwhelming, coming out of nowhere. There was no rhyme or reason to them. She knew she could try and be rational and think herself out of them. But she couldn't stop the heave in her chest, or the overwhelming feelings of not being good enough. They were swamping her, making it almost difficult to breathe.

'Cora?' There was instant concern on Jonas's face.

She stood up and shook her head, trying to breathe and stammer the words out. 'I…don't feel up to dinner tonight. I can't do this. I think it's best if I just go back to the hotel.'

He looked at her as if those words had stung, and she knew instantly it was the delivery. She hadn't added the word 'alone' to her dialogue, but her tone had made certain the implication was there.

He reached for her hand. 'No. Don't go. I wanted tonight to be special. I wanted to talk to you. What's wrong?'

The words just erupted from her belly. 'Nothing. Everything. I don't know.' She held out her shaking arms, letting the paper cup of *glögg* fall at her feet. She looked around her at the people, families, and all the signs of

Christmas in every part of the square. Even though she knew they were outside, it was as if the walls were pressing in all around her. She couldn't breathe. She couldn't be here. She couldn't do this.

She turned and ran, ignoring the fact her clumpy boots slowed her pace. If her head had been straight, she would have gone back to the hotel. But nothing was making sense to her right now. Every corner she turned seemed to take her to another festooned street. Christmas lights and decorations had never bothered her quite as much as they did now.

Flashes appeared in her head. Holding her mum's cold hand. One minute she'd been there, full of life and laughing, and the next minute she'd been gone. Nothing could save her. Then the flash of her father's withered face on the pillow, his pallor sicklier than any shade of white or grey. The laboured breaths and wheeze. And the memories of hating every second of seeing the bright, vibrant man that she loved in pain. The cancer had come quickly after her mum had died, and Cora always thought he'd had no strength to fight because his heart was already broken. It was agonising, but that was what was left in her memory. And over the years it had grown bigger, instead of fading. It had pushed all the best memories out of place. And with it was the overwhelming sensation that Cora had failed both of her parents.

The final breath had been a relief to them both, and, for that as well, the guilt was overwhelming.

Cora had reached the harbour now, panting, and, catching hold of the barrier in front of her, she clung on, knowing there was nowhere left to run.

She didn't even hear his footsteps, but knew instantly the arm around her was his. For a few moments he didn't speak, just stood with his chest against her back, his arms around her, and his own rapid breaths matching her own.

'I hate seeing you like this. Tell me what's wrong, Cora. I want to help.'

She couldn't find the words; exhaustion was sweeping over her.

He turned her around to face him. 'I wanted this night to be good between us. I wanted to talk about what comes next.' There were deep furrows across his brow, and he was clutching her array of shopping bags in his hand.

'What comes next is, I get on a plane and go home. Isn't it a bit late to have the "what about us?" talk?' It came out much more bitterly than she wanted it to. But her heart was aching. Every moment felt like another realisation. If he'd wanted to talk about them, shouldn't it have been mentioned long before now?

He hesitated, and it made her heart plummet inside her chest. 'I was waiting,' he said cautiously.

'Waiting for what?'

She saw him swallow awkwardly. 'I thought they were going to offer you the job today.'

Those feelings that she was trying hard to push away swamped her again. They hadn't wanted her. She wasn't good enough to be offered the job.

His pale eyes looked fraught with worry, and she wasn't quite sure how to read it. 'Well, they didn't. But, so what? Why would that make a difference to any talk about us?'

She stepped away from him. 'What? Can there only be an "us" if I'm right here? On your doorstep, where it's convenient? Is that why you waited to have this discussion? And now I've told you that they haven't offered me the job, I can see how awkward you feel. I take it that rules out any discussion for us at all?' She put her hand on her chest. 'How am I supposed to feel? Has this all just been a convenience for you? Because it hasn't been for me. And now I'm finding out just how important I am in your life. I won't be working here. I'll be back in London. I've been here for a while now, Jonas. We could have had the "what about us?" conversation at any point.'

The words were coming out so quickly, she almost couldn't breathe. 'And today? Tonight?' She let out a hollow laugh. 'It couldn't be more fitting. This is my worst time of year. You nearly had me fooled for that too—that I should try and create new Christmas memories. But how can I do that? No matter where I am in this world, I'm always going to feel like this—alone.' She closed her eyes, hating herself for spilling everything out to him. Her voice shook. 'You've no idea how much I hate this date. This is the date that my mum died from an aortic aneurysm after going into hospital with back pain. A year and a day later, my dad died from cancer on Christmas Eve. And things don't get better with time—no matter what well-meaning people say. They just amplify and haunt me. How can I create new memories when the bad ones take me over— no matter how hard I try?'

Her shoulders started to shake. Jonas had his arms around her instantly, propping her up, taking her weight as her legs started to crumple. 'Let me help you, Cora. Let me help you. We can get through this together. You should have told me. I had no idea how hard this was for you.' His eyes glanced towards the bags he gripped in his hands—her bags. And there it was again. That weird look.

And his earlier words didn't soothe her, they just injected her with a force of solid determination. He still hadn't said the words that mattered most. And now, she realised, she didn't want him to. She didn't want him to react to this situation by saying something he didn't actually feel. He'd never given her a true indication that he wanted a long-term relationship with her. Her heart twisted in her chest. She loved this man, but it was clear he didn't have the same strong feelings that she did. It was easier to end things here and now and walk away with a bit of her dignity intact. But something inside her flared as she saw his eyes still fixed on the bags.

'Why do you do that?' she snapped.

'What?' He looked confused.

'You.' She thrust her hand towards him. 'Every time you see one of my shopping bags you get a weird look on your face. I know you don't like shopping, Jonas, but you really need to get over yourself. People all around the world shop!' She'd thrown her arms upwards now and the expression on Jonas's face changed, filling with hurt and regret.

He took a deep breath. 'I'm sorry,' he said slowly. 'The bags just reminded me of a past experience. Every time I see them, it just takes me back.'

Her eyes narrowed. 'What past experience?'

He shook his head. 'An ex, with spending habits that left me in a world of debt. Every time I saw you clutching shopping bags, it brought back memories.'

Her brow wrinkled. 'That's ridiculous. Why on earth would I leave you in debt with my shopping? I have more than enough money of my own.'

Her brain was spinning. Was this the mysterious ex she'd heard a few of his colleagues hint at? One had even mentioned they'd thought Jonas might have planned on asking her to marry him.

Every part of her body bristled. He'd never mentioned his ex to her before. He'd never confided in Cora, and that made her realise that he'd never taken their relationship that seriously.

As the thoughts churned in her brain he nodded and closed his eyes. 'And when you say it like that, I seem like a complete fool. But I couldn't stop the memories, and it became more about my bad judgement than anything else.'

She stepped back as a cold wave of realisation swept over her. Nothing about this had

been us it seemed. Maybe the connection between them had all been in her head?

She straightened and looked at him. 'I'm
going home, Jonas. I'm going home tomorrow.
I'm sorry that they didn't offer me that job, but,
in a way, I'm not. Because now I know. Now I
know this would never have worked between
us. And it's better this way. It has to be.'

She turned quickly, walking swiftly back
towards the centre.

He was alongside her in an instant. 'Cora,
stop, let me talk to you. Don't walk away. I
don't want things to be like this between us.'

She stopped walking for a second and looked
him in the eye. 'This is exactly how things
are between us, Jonas, which is exactly why I
should leave. Now, stop.' She held up one hand.
'Leave me alone. I can't be anywhere near you
right now.' She took a deep breath. 'I'm going
to keep walking, and you—' she pointed at his
chest '—are going to leave me alone.'

And she started walking as quickly as she
could—even though her vision was blinded
with tears and her heart ached.

All she could do was keep walking. Right
on back to London. She'd wanted to trust
him with her heart, but it was clear that she
couldn't.

CHAPTER FOURTEEN

HE WAS AN IDIOT. He was an absolute prize idiot. The words had been on the tip of his tongue last night—even before he'd noticed she was crying—and he half wished he'd blurted out the *I love you* as soon as he'd seen her.

Instead, he'd been distracted by the pile of shopping bags around her feet. And in that moment of distraction, which had made him think about bad memories, he'd lost his momentum and opportunity.

The way Cora had looked at him last night had been like a knife to the heart. Had he totally misread everything? She'd seemed almost cold. He couldn't help but wonder if she'd always meant to break up with him—had never considered anything serious between them. If that were true, his *I love you* would have been sadly misplaced and awkward for them both.

Although he'd wanted to run after her last night, her story about why she was so sad at

Christmas had floored him. He'd known it was something significant. But the look in her eyes when she'd told him about losing both her mum and dad so close to Christmas, one year after the next, would have broken the heart of the coldest ice man. And when she'd told him to let her walk away, even though every cell in his body had protested, he'd known he had to listen. And his head had filled with crazy doubts. Maybe Cora had only ever wanted a temporary fling. Even with the potential job offer, she might just have been placating him. Letting him think she would consider it, when she really just wanted to head back to London and get on with her life.

He still couldn't believe that she *hadn't* been offered it. And it almost felt as if she'd blamed him for that too last night. Or maybe his head was just too full of conflicting emotions to actually think straight.

So, he'd let her walk away. If she didn't love him, then this was for the best.

But it had been an achingly long night. He hadn't been able to sleep for a minute. He'd played things over and over in his head. What if he'd done something different? What if he'd chased after her when she'd walked away, and admitted that he loved her?

He'd been in work since six a.m.—after toying with the idea to walk to the hotel and deciding not to. He would wait for her here. It was her last day in Sweden. He wanted her to come into work, say goodbye to the friends she'd made, and then he would ask if he could have some of her time.

He wanted to wear his heart on his sleeve and tell her that he absolutely loved and adored her. That last night, he'd had a special gift for her in his pocket. He wanted to tell her that was what his plans had been. A nice restaurant. Some good food. Some wine. And a chance to tell the woman he loved that he wanted to spend the rest of his life with her.

He only prayed she would still let him.

The clock ticked past in slow motion. He paced near the unit. He paced near the labour suite. He paced near the paediatric ward. But Cora was nowhere. He asked and asked, but no one had seen her.

He wandered the management corridors, wondering if she'd been called to some kind of meeting. He still couldn't believe she hadn't been offered the job. But it had never even entered Jonas's head that Cora would consider that part of a reason to be together. He'd already decided last night that if Cora wanted to return to London, he'd ask if he could join her.

But he had to find her first.

A colleague had asked him to verify some documents for him, and Jonas scribbled his signature and passport details, before ramming his passport in his back pocket and pacing the corridors again.

Alice came and found him in the corridor. Her face was sad. 'She's not here.'

'I know she's not here. I've been looking everywhere.'

Alice sighed and put her hand on Jonas's arm. 'Did you message her?'

'Of course, I did.' It came out much more snappily than intended.

Alice pressed her lips together and gave an understanding slow nod. 'Well, she texted me.'

His head shot up. 'What? What did she say? Where is she?'

Alice's voice was soft. 'At the airport. Her flight leaves in the next two hours.'

'What?' Panic gripped straight across his chest like a vice.

He looked around madly.

'You'll need to be quick,' she whispered.

Jonas didn't hesitate. He grabbed his car keys, his jacket and started to run.

His car was in the car park at the hospital. It was the middle of the day, so traffic wasn't too heavy in Stockholm, and he did his best to stick to the speed limit on the way to Arlanda airport.

By the time he reached the airport, the slow entry to the car park and the excruciating line of people trying to file into a parking space made him want to explode. He dived out of the car, and raced to the airport entrance doors, his eyes immediately scanning the boards for her flight. Some part of him felt a wave of panic when he couldn't initially find a flight to London. Then he realised. LHR—Heathrow. The abbreviation had thrown him.

He ran towards the security entrance, scanning all people sitting in chairs, around the washrooms and in the stores along the way. There was no sign of Cora.

As he reached the security entrance, one of the guards eyed him suspiciously. 'Ticket?' he asked.

Of course. He didn't get past here without a ticket. 'Can I put a call out for someone?'

It was as if the man could read his mind. He raised an eyebrow. 'Will they come if we call them?'

His stomach clenched. He darted back through the crowds of people slowly milling about the airport as if they had all the time in the world, straight to one of the ticket desks.

He slammed his credit card on the counter. 'I need a ticket.'

'Where to?' asked the girl behind the desk, pulling back a little.

'Anywhere,' was his instant response.

Her brow furrowed and she gave him a suspicious glance. Just what he needed—her to call security, and him to get ejected from the airport.

'The love of my life is in the departure lounge. I need to get in there—and to do that I need a ticket.'

'The love of your life?' The girl gave him a hard stare.

Jonas nodded then screwed up his face. 'I just haven't told her that yet.'

The girl's eyebrows raised. 'Are you asking her to stay, or do you want to go with her?'

'What?'

'You said you need a ticket. Wouldn't it be wise to buy a ticket to the same place, instead of just any ticket?' She didn't wait for him to respond—just continued with her hard stare as she folded her arms. 'After all—you can't just expect her to come back home with you. If you love her, you have to be prepared to go where she is.'

Even though he didn't have time for this, and his heart was currently racing, he leaned forward and smiled at the girl. 'You're that kind of quirky character in the movie, aren't you? The one that almost stops the guy reaching his girl?'

She nodded. 'What can I say?' She made a sign with her fingers, 'Hashtag, team girl. Have you any idea how many stories like this I hear from hapless guys who just haven't got their act together?'

'Okay, I'm a shameful, pathetic human being. Now let me buy a ticket to London Heathrow and send me on my way.'

She gave him an approving nod, took his credit card and passport and her fingers flew across the keyboard. A minute later she handed him a printed boarding card, and a receipt. She sighed and said, 'Okay then, go be a hero and don't screw this up.'

'Thank you.' The words had barely left his mouth when he started running back through the hall towards the security check area.

He thrust his boarding card towards security.

The queue seemed to deliberately crawl forward. Pat-downs took for ever. Jonas was watching the clock on the wall behind the check-in desk; it seemed to be on fast forward. He could also see a board filled with flight information. The boarding gate number was up

for Cora's flight, along with the flashing words
Go to Gate.

He was a few seconds away from pleading
with the people ahead to let him skip the queue
when another checkpoint was opened and a
guard waved him over. He'd never moved so
fast. He stuck his belongings in the tray to be
security scanned, held his hands out to be patted down, collected his tray, pushed his shoes
on his feet and rammed everything else in his
pockets, and then he started running all over
again in the direction of the gate.

A few people shot him an amused glance
as he sprinted past. The message on the flight
screen had now changed. *Now Boarding*. There
were already a few people in the line.

He ran straight to the front, ignoring the
glares and craning his neck to see the few people who'd already walked into the tunnel to
board the plane. He didn't recognise any jackets. He took long strides and looked at every
face in the waiting line. Nope. None of them
were Cora.

He turned back and ran to the front again.
'Can you check a name for me to see if they've
gone through to the plane?'

The attendant, who was scanning someone's
ticket, didn't even look up. 'Go to the back of
the line, please, sir.'

He wanted to argue. But that wouldn't do any good. He'd only get thrown out, and right now he needed to be in this airport, in the departure lounge.

His brain kept whirring. Maybe he should go back and check the shops? She might still be shopping.

He darted back and scanned the nearest tourist souvenir shop, the duty free, a perfume shop and a bakery and coffee shop. No Cora. No sign anywhere.

There was a buzz.

'Last call for Flight G654 to London Heathrow. Would the last remaining passengers make their way to the boarding gate now?'

When he ran back along the corridor, he was suddenly very conscious that there was absolutely no one waiting to board. There was only one attendant, glancing at her watch and looking slightly annoyed.

His brain freaked for a moment. What if Cora had changed her mind and gone back to Stockholm? Could he really take that chance? He might end up on a flight for no reason.

But he couldn't take the chance. Not for a second. Not when Cora was at stake. Worst-case scenario, he would end up on a flight for no reason and have to take one back.

He handed his boarding card over and walked

down the longest flight bridge in the world. He hadn't even looked at his seat number.

The air attendant smiled and gestured to him to walk down the entire length of the plane. He could hear the door being closed behind him, but all he could do was scan the faces in the seats. As he got nearer and nearer to the back of the plane, his heart sank. He couldn't see her dark hair anywhere.

He got to the last row, and someone lifted their head.

A head with dark hair. Cora. She had been rummaging in her bag that was shoved under her seat. Jonas couldn't believe it. He glanced at his ticket. Then slid into the seat next to her.

She sat up straight away. And he realised she must have recognised his aftershave.

Her face was shocked. 'What are you doing here?'

She looked around as if it were some kind of bad joke. But no, the doors to the plane were closed, and the plane had started to taxi to the runway.

'I came to find you.'

Her face grew tight. 'But why?'

'Because I didn't get a chance to say the things to you that I should have.'

She blinked and waited a few seconds. 'And what should you have said?'

'That I love you, I'm crazy about you and I want to be where you are. And I don't care if that's London, Stockholm or anywhere else.'

She drew in a shaky breath and shook her head a little. 'I'm on my way back to London, Jonas. Why tell me now?'

'Because I'm an idiot. Because I was scared. Because I let myself get tied up in past experiences, because the truth is, for me, you were just too good to be true.'

'You got on a plane to tell me this?' There was an edge to her voice, and the last thing he wanted to do was upset her. He had a purpose for being here and had to get to the point.

'I waited all morning for you at the hospital. I was stupid enough to think you might show up at work today. I wanted to come to the hotel this morning, but thought that was just too creepy.'

The corners of her lips edged up for a second.

But they went back again as she slowed her breathing. 'I've been here for seven weeks, we got closer and closer, and you never told me that you loved me, you never really talked about the future—just danced around the subject.'

He reached over and put his hand over hers as the plane lifted off from the runway. 'You're right. And I'm sorry. But don't leave like this. I don't want you to leave like this. If you go, I go. I can't imagine not waking up next to you in the morning. This morning was the worst ever. To turn over and find a big empty space was the worst feeling in the world. I kept telling myself that I'd see you at the hospital. I'd talk to you. I'd persuade you to give me a chance to explain. Tell you all the things I should have told you last night before you walked away. Then Alice told me about your text.'

'She was texting me literally every hour, on the hour.'

'She never told me that.'

Cora raised an eyebrow. 'She's a very persuasive, persistent woman.'

She shook her head again. 'But your whole life is in Stockholm, Jonas. What on earth will you do in London?'

He kept his face grave. 'My whole life will be wherever you are, Cora. If you'll let me.' He slipped his hand into his pocket. 'I didn't get it. Your whole Christmas feeling. When you told me last night, you broke my heart, because I just wanted to be there for you.'

She closed her eyes and spoke quietly. 'And I pushed you away. Because that's what I've learned to do. I don't talk about it with anyone. Most of my colleagues back home already know—so no one brings it up. I just volunteer for the Christmas shifts, and no one asks why.' She lowered her head. 'I got so used to not telling anyone, that I just couldn't cope last night. I was overwhelmed.' She kept her head down, but squeezed his hand. 'You told me to try and make new Christmas memories, and I did. I started to. I started to make them with you. Then I felt guilty. That I didn't deserve to make them, and I was betraying my mum and dad by even considering moving on.' She looked up in surprise when Jonas wiped away a tear that slid down her cheek.

'We don't ever have to do Christmas, Cora. If you don't want to, then that's fine with me. We can take holidays and go off to some remote cabin for a few days and just be ourselves, just chill. Take some time away from everything.'

She shook her head and breathed deeply. 'No, Jonas. I'm going to do what I should have done years ago. I'm going to go to a counsellor and talk my way through this. Maybe I'll never feel better, but I have to try.' She gave a soft smile. 'Maybe I should try to make new memories.'

He stroked her cheek with his finger. 'And I want to be by your side. Whatever your decision, it will be fine with me. What I have with you is too special that I can't even contemplate a life where we're not together. I've never loved someone the way I love you. Not even close.'

By now the plane had climbed high into the sky. Cora glanced out of the window. 'You're actually coming to London? You know today is Christmas Eve?' There was still a wave of sadness in her eyes.

'And this is a day you shouldn't be on your own. I'm happy to fade into the background and give you space, or, equally, just give you lots of hugs.'

Cora didn't cry. She just laid her head on his shoulder. He whispered into her hair. 'I'm hoping a really kind-hearted woman will let me bunk up with her tonight, and maybe for a whole lot longer.'

'You really don't want to go back to Stockholm?'

'I can be a midwife anywhere,' he answered promptly, and he truly meant it.

'And I can be a doctor anywhere too,' she said simply.

'Then the world is our oyster.'

She nodded as the air attendant approached with drinks for them both. As she set them down, Jonas reached for the item he'd taken from his pocket. 'My timing isn't great. But I had something for you.' He smiled. 'I bought it a few weeks ago, but wanted to give it to you the day before you left—without realising what I was doing.'

She took a sip of her wine and wrinkled her nose. 'What is it?'

'It's a message.' His voice was steady. 'Things are a bit different in Sweden. You might think we do things in reverse.' He swallowed and flipped open the small velvet box. 'In the older days in Sweden, this was an engagement ring.'

Cora leaned forward, her eyes wide at the simple gold band, with a thicker one next to it.

'We both wear them,' he said steadily.

She hadn't said anything yet, and his nerves were making him fill the gap. 'I promise I'll buy you a diamond later—but we usually save them for the actual wedding.'

Her eyes were wide as she turned to face him. 'What exactly are you asking me?'

Jonas didn't hesitate for a second. 'I'm asking you to marry me, Cora, and pick where we live together. I love you. I was a fool not to tell you sooner, but I promise I'll spend the rest of my life telling you every day.'

Her finger brushed the gold rings in the box. She smiled. 'Aren't I supposed to buy you a ring?'

'I decided to save us some time.'

She kept staring at him in wonder. 'When did you buy these?'

He groaned. 'Will you just answer the darn question?' He'd drunk some of the wine given to them by the air attendant, but if she didn't give him an answer soon, he couldn't swear it would stay down. No one ever spoke about how nerve-racking it was for a guy to ask the woman he loved the biggest question in the world and wait for an answer.

She slid one hand up the side of his face and through his hair, pulling him towards her. Just as their lips were about to touch she gave him his answer. 'Yes,' she whispered.

And they kissed, forgetting about the world outside and concentrating only on each other.

EPILOGUE

'READY?' CORA GRINNED at Jonas as he tugged at the kilt she'd made him wear.

'Is this supposed to be comfortable?' he asked, straightening up.

'Absolutely not.' She kept smiling. 'You're supposed to spend the whole night in terror that you'll turn too quickly and the whole world will see what they're not supposed to.'

He shook his head. 'I'm not sure about all this "true Scotsman" tale. Did you make it up? Because I can tell you right now that any Norseman with this on would wear boxers.'

She walked up and put her hands on the lapels of his Highland jacket. 'But tonight, husband, you are an honorary Scotsman.' She winked. 'And you did lose the bet.'

He sighed and grabbed his wallet, stuffing it into his sporran. 'I never thought you'd hold me to it.'

'You're quite hundsome as a Scotsman. Maybe we should try this more often.'

Jonas let out a disgruntled noise as he grabbed her hand. 'Let's go before this Christmas party starts without you.'

Cora took a final glance in the mirror at her floor-length red satin gown, grabbed her purse and made her way down the hotel corridor with her new husband.

They'd married quietly, only a few days before, with her sister as bridesmaid, and Jonas's friend as best man. Their reception would be held back in Sweden after Christmas. All their friends and colleagues back at Stockholm City should have received their invites in the mail today.

They'd arrived in London nearly a year before and as soon as they'd landed Cora had received the call from Stockholm City asking her to be Head of Neonatal Intensive Care.

She'd accepted immediately, then spent the few days after celebrating with Jonas, before packing up her things, renting out her flat and moving to Stockholm permanently.

Tonight was a double celebration. Their wedding, and the Royal Kensington Christmas party to celebrate the achievements of all the staff who'd been part of the Kensington project over the last fifty years. Organising had been a logistical nightmare, but Cora had taken on the challenge with pride after Chris Taylor had asked her to. Her first calls had been to her fellow three Kensington Project recipients that year. It seemed that the project had had a big impact on all of their lives. Tonight, she would get to see some of them for the first time in nearly a year.

The large ballroom in the hotel was decorated with green boughs and red bows.

Pictures of all those chosen to be part of the Kensington Project over the years lined the walls. Chloe, Scott, and Stella all stared back at her with pride on their faces. Cora glanced quickly at the four people who'd had the honour this year, wondering if their lives would change as much as her and her colleagues' lives had.

A waiter was standing in the entranceway with a silver tray of glasses filled with champagne. Cora had only taken a few steps when Chloe ran over and threw her arms around her. Chloe's green dress was gorgeous and her curly hair was piled up on her head.

'What took you? Aren't you staying here, same as us?'

Cora nodded and gestured to Jonas. 'My husband needed a hand with his kilt. It seems he's not used to wearing a skirt.' She kept hugging Chloe tightly. 'You look fabulous. Are we still on for tomorrow so I get to see this gorgeous baby?'

Chloe grinned, her eyes sparkling at the mention of the baby she'd had back in July. 'Can't wait. We'll meet you at St James's Park.'

A deep laugh sounded behind them as Chloe's husband stepped out from behind her to put a kiss on Cora's cheek. Sam, the general surgeon from Kingston Memorial who'd captured Chloe's heart, automatically started teasing Jonas. 'Don't bend over too quickly.' He laughed good-naturedly.

'Hey, don't start this party without me.' Stella, their colleague from Orthopaedics, glowed in a silver fringed dress as she wrapped an arm around both of them. With her dark bob, she looked as if she'd stepped straight out of a nineteen-twenties movie.

'You look fantastic,' said Cora, kissing her cheek. 'I wasn't sure if you'd want to make the journey from Toronto.' Like herself, Stella had decided to relocate after meeting Aiden and his small son when she'd travelled to Toronto as part of the Kensington Project.

She reached out to shake Aiden's hand.

'Where's Scott?' asked Chloe.

'Right behind me,' said Stella as she nodded over her shoulder.

They watched as Scott, their handsome American cardiology colleague, danced his way across the floor to them, his arm around his wife, Fliss. He clinked glasses with them all as soon as he arrived.

The girls all wrapped arms around each other and started to laugh and joke, ordering a bottle of champagne from a passing waiter and sitting down at a table to exchange stories.

As the music started a little while later, all four men appeared on cue to take their partners onto the dance floor.

Cora slid into her new husband's arms and wrapped her arms around his neck as the slow Christmas song started.

'Happy?' he asked.

'Delighted,' she whispered. 'And this year, I get to have my first Christmas Day in Stockholm. I can't wait to make a whole host of new memories to keep for ever.'

Cora had been seeing a counsellor back in Stockholm and was slowly unpicking her feelings of guilt and grief. Jonas was with her every step of the way, and she'd never been happier.

'So, what are our plans for tomorrow?' he asked. They only had another few days in London before flying home again.

'We're meeting a gorgeous baby, and then...'

she gave him a special smile '… I have a few ideas about what we could get up to.'

He looked at her with amused suspicion. 'And what might that be?'

She spun around under his arm before pressing up against him. 'What do you think of this dress?'

Jonas's eyes ran appreciatively down the figure-hugging floor-length red dress. 'I adore it. Is this a trick?'

'Could be. My plans include doing my best to ensure I don't fit into this dress next year. But I might need some help with that.'

He spun her around the dance floor. 'Oh, I think I can help with that. I think we should practise.' He dipped her low, then pulled her back up. 'Let's do our best to expand this family.'

And Cora stood on her tiptoes and planted a kiss on her husband's lips. 'That, darling, is music to my ears.'

And they danced their way around the floor again.

* * * * *

If you missed the previous story in
The Christmas Project quartet,
then check out

Winter Nights with the Single Dad
by Allie Kincheloe

And if you missed the previous stories
in The Christmas Project quartet,
then check out

Christmas Miracle in Jamaica
by Ann McIntosh
December Reunion in Central Park
by Deanne Anders

All available now!